Richard Cumberland

False Impressions

A Comedy in Five Acts. Performed at the Theatre Royal, Covent Garden

Richard Cumberland

False Impressions
A Comedy in Five Acts. Performed at the Theatre Royal, Covent Garden

ISBN/EAN: 9783744767224

Printed in Europe, USA, Canada, Australia, Japan

Cover: Foto ©Andreas Hilbeck / pixelio.de

More available books at **www.hansebooks.com**

FALSE IMPRESSIONS:

A

C O M E D Y

IN FIVE ACTS.

PERFORMED

At the Theatre Royal, Covent Garden.

✠✠✠✠✠✠✠✠✠✠✠✠✠

By RICHARD CUMBERLAND, Esq.

Sæpe, etiam audacem, fugat hoc terretque poëtam;
Quod numero plures, virtute et honore minores,
Indocti, ſtolidique et depugnare parati
Si diſcordet eques, media inter carmina poſcunt
Aut urſum aut pugiles: his nam plebecula gaudet.

✠✠✠✠✠✠✠✠✠✠✠✠✠✠✠✠✠✠✠✠✠✠✠✠✠✠✠✠✠

London:
PRINTED FOR C. DILLY, IN THE POULTRY, 1797.

[*Price* 2*s.*]

PROLOGUE.

Spoken by Mr. *MURRAY.*

THE time hath been, but in a barbarous age,
  When poets brav'd their audience from the ftage,
Poets pontifical, whofe lofty tone
Acknowledg'd no tribunal but their own,
And fent their Prologue-purveyor to raife
Firft fruits and fines of tributary praife.

Our modern bards are taught an humbler ftrain,
And, if lefs valiant, are not half fo vain ;
No longer aim the nation's tafte to lead,
Content if they can follow and fucceed.
Thus if the time fhould come, when in the place
Of Nature you fhou'd fubftitute grimace,
(Fatal reverfe !) What cou'd the Poet do?
Offend the many to appeafe the few ?
No, if in Greece true tafte had been as fcarce,
The Stagyrite himfelf had ftood for farce.
If wit thro' five long acts will not hold out,
Momus muft help to ftir the laugh about,
And when you crown his mummery with applaufe,
You bribe him to tranfgrefs the drama's laws.

He were a very wild romantic elf,
Who only wrote to figure on the fhelf;
To hear his own fad fentiments rebound
Thro' empty galleries with a dying found,
And fit like Seneca in calm decay,
Watching how life fteals drop by drop away :
No, let him take his profit and his eafe,
And trifle on fo long as trifles pleafe :
Too weak to ftruggle againft fafhion's tide,
If with the current he's content to glide,
He only yields as Cæfar did before,
When Tiber's torrent drove him from the fhore.

The fimple tale we have to tell this night,
Shews truth triumphant over ranc'rous fpite,
Cafts in dark fhades the bafe defamer's part,
And crowns with juft reward the liberal heart.
Oh might our efforts gain their wifht-for end,
The gay to' amufe, the faulty to amend,
Make fiction rule her thoughts by nature's laws,
And wit exert her powers in virtue's caufe,
Then and then only might we claim applaufe.

Dramatis Perſonæ.

SIR OLIVER MONTRATH - -   MR. MURRAY.

ALGERNON - - - - - -   MR. HOLMAN.

SCUD (an Apothecary) - - -   MR. QUICK.

EARLING (an Attorney) - - -   MR. WHITFIELD.

SIMON SINGLE (an old Servant)   MR. MUNDEN.

FARMER GAWDRY - - - -   MR. DAVENPORT.

ISAAC (his Son) - - - - -   MR. FOLLET.

PETER (Journeyman to SCUD) -   MR. ABBOT.

JACK (a Boy) - - - - - -   MR. SIMMONS.

FRANK (a Footman) - - - -   MR. THOMPSON.

LADY CYPRESS - - - - -   MISS CHAPMAN.

EMILY FITZALLAN - - -   MISS BETTERTON.

JENNY SCUD - - - - -   MRS. KNIGHT.

MRS. BUCKRAM - - - - -   MRS. DAVENPORT.

RACHEL WILLIAMS - - -   MRS. NORTON.

FALSE IMPRESSIONS:

A

COMEDY.

ACT I.

SCENE, *a Chamber in the House of* SCUD
the Apothecary.

Enter SCUD.

AHA! very good, very good. Here I am
again—no bad night's work—pretty fairish
job—patient none the better, myself none the
worse—tipt two guineas for fitting up with old
Lady Cyprefs—flept comfortably in an easy chair—
nibbled a cold chicken with my Lady's woman—
tiff'd a can of flip with the old butler—crib'd a kifs
or two from the sweet lips of Mrs. Rachel, and
gave her a box of cardamums and a bottle of elder-
flower water in return for the favour—So far, fo
good—Well done, Jerry Scud!—Holloa! Jack,
boy, puppy! where are you?

Enter JACK.

Jack. Here am I, master.

Scud. Fetch my flippers, firrah! Take off my
boots.   [*Exit* JACK.
My dear Jenny can't abide boots; very right,
very reafonable; foil the carpet, dawb her petti-
coats, annoy her olfactories—No wonder—delicate

B   darling

darling my Jenny—ſweet pretty creature—perfect
poſey of a woman—   [*Re-enter* JACK.
So, ſo, ſo! take hold, ſirrah; pull away ! That will
do, that will do—ſet my ſlippers—red moroccos—
ſtockings not ſoil'd—pretty well off-there—Now,
puppy Jack, where's your miſtreſs?

Jack. Don't know.

Scud. How does ſhe do?

Jack. Can't tell.

Scud. Is ſhe at home?

Jack. An't ſure.

Scud. Was ſhe at home laſt night, or was ſhe out?

Jack. Both: ſometimes in, ſometimes out.

Scud. You're a fool. Had ſhe company?

Jack. No, no; no company.

Scud. Poor dear Jenny! What, quite alone?

Jack. No, no; not quite alone.

Scud. Jackanapes, didn't you tell me ſhe had
no company?

Jack. Yes I did; becauſe why? ſhe bade me let
no company in; yet ſhe wasn't quite alone by herſelf, becauſe young Squire Algernon was alone
with her.

Scud. The devil and his dam! I'm done for.
Get out of my ſight! begone! away with you!

                    [*Exit* JACK.

Ah Jenny, Jenny, Jenny! You are bent upon
ſending your poor huſband to heaven ſome day or
other, when it rains while the ſun ſhines—How
now, Peter!

                    PETER *enters.*

Peter. Is there any alteration to be made in Lady
Cypreſs's medicines?

                                        Scud.

Scud. None at all, none; draughts *ficut ante.*

Peter. They do no good.

Scud. They do no harm.

Peter. They are a mere chip in porridge—Conferve of rofes will never cure an afthma.

Scud. I know it; what then ? A patient cur'd is a cuftomer loft. In one word therefore, *repetatur hauftus.*

Peter. Be it fo! let nature do the work herfelf; our practice wont puzzle her. [*Exit* PETER.

Scud. Miferable man that I am; my Jenny tête-a-tête with Harry Algernon !—a rake, a rogue, a rantipole. Hah ! here fhe comes—

Enter Mrs. SCUD.

Light of my eyes, joy of my heart, fair as a lily, come to my arms ! Out all night—figh'd for my darling—counted the minutes—terrible long abfence—how did you bear it ?—Doubt you've been lonefome—

Jenny. Not at all ; far from it. Harry Algernon has been here.

Scud. What does he want ? Nothing to fay to him.

Jenny. But you'll hear what he has to fay to you.

Scud. Let him fay it to me only. Not fit company for jewel Jenny.

Jenny. Ridiculous ! He only wants a little of your intereft with Lady Cyprefs.—Apropos ! he has brought you half a buck.

Scud. Let him take his half buck home again. Wou'dn't name his name to Lady Cyprefs for all the venifon in his father's park.

Jenny. Hav'n't you nam'd his name to Lady

B 2 Cyprefs ?

Cyprefs ? I doubt you have, Jerry, oftener than you ought, and in a way you fhou'd be afham'd of.

Scud. Only faid what lawyer Earling faid—always had the law o' my fide.

Jenny. On which fide was truth ? on which fide was gratitude ? Recollect yourfelf.

Scud. What fhou'd I recollect ?

Jenny. I'll tell you.—Your adventure at Barnftable races, when in the pride of your heart you muft fhew off in your new gig forfooth ; and where wou'd you have been now if the very man you have defam'd hadn't fav'd your life at the peril of his own ?

Scud. He did, he did—I don't deny it. Tit run reftive—tipt me over a wheelbarrow—tumbled under his heels—might have been kick'd to atoms—furgeon's work as it was—fnapt my arm—well it was not my neck—much obliged to Harry Algernon—never fpoke againft him fince.

Jenny. Speak for him, man ; 'tisn't enough you do not fpeak againft him : liberate your confcience.

Scud. Jenny, Jenny, liberate my confcience, as you call it, and I fhall liberate my cuftomers ; if Harry Algernon will be a rantipole ; if his women and his wine, his racing and his revelling, have crofs'd him out of the old lady's books, how am I to blame ?

Jenny. Well, well, 'tisn't your bufinefs to fet the worft fide of his character to view ; you have benefited by his courage and humanity—why don't you talk of them, and hold your tongue about his frailties ?

Scud. My tongue can do nobody any harm.

I tell

I tell you it is all up with him: lawyer Earling has done his bufinefs. If ever he enters my lady's doors, or touches a fhilling of her fortune while he breathes, fet me down for a fool and a falfe prophet.

Jenny. Suppofe he does not aim at touching a fhilling of her fortune; fuppofe he only wants— but here he comes, and will tell you what he wants.

ALGERNON *enters.*

Alg. Ah, Jerry, my worthy fellow, give me your hand, give me your help.—No, no, that's not the point at prefent—take your fingers off my pulfe.

Scud. Very high, let me tell you—very full— gallops at a furious rate.

Alg. Expectation raifes it, hope quickens it; love is my difeafe; and if you don't ftand my friend, difappointment will be my death.

Scud. Love! Can't cure love—troubled enough to cure the confequences of it.

Alg. Hark ye, Jerry, you are an intimate of Lady Cyprefs; I, though her neareft of kin, am an exile. Within her caftle lives the idol of my foul, Emily Fitzallan; obtain for me an interview with her, and though you can't cure love, you may refcue me from death, and then you may fairly boaft of having fav'd one man's life by your practice.

Scud. Can't do't—not poffible—fair Emily never goes out of the caftle.

Alg. Therefore it is I want to go into it.

Scud. Hopelefs cafe—not upon the chances— Old Lady won't bear to look upon you.

Alg. I'll excufe her if I may but look upon the young one: manage that for me, my good fellow.—

Nobody

Nobody knows me; nobody can find me out; I'm a ſtranger to the whole family.

Scud. And ſo you are likely to remain.

Jenny. Come, come, Jerry, caſt about; be good natur'd, and contrive ſome errand or pretence to introduce him. If there is a little danger, ſurely you may riſque it for the preſerver of your life.

Scud. Fooliſh ſcheme, jewel Jenny, fooliſh ſcheme.—Won't do.

Alg. Have you no medicines to ſend in? Can't I perſonate your peſtle and mortar-man?

Scud. Not you; I keep no ſuch peſtle and mortar-man in my ſhop.

Alg. But you keep a heart in your body, and a memory in your brains, therefore you muſt ſtand for me as I have ſtood for you.

Jenny. Huſh! here comes Simon Single, the keeper of the caſtle. Leave me with him, and I warrant I have a key to his caſtle.

Alg. Angel of my hope, into your hands I commit my cauſe.

Scud. Aye, aye, leave your cauſe, and quit your company.   [*Exeunt* SCUD *and* ALGERNON.

SIMON SINGLE, JENNY SCUD.

Jenny. Welcome, welcome, my good friend!

Simon. Glad to ſee you, pretty Mrs. Jane.

Jenny. So you are taking your rounds this fair morning, Mr. Simon.

Simon. Better take them than Jerry's doſes.

Jenny. I agree with you.

Simon. So wou'd not they perhaps.

Jenny. And how are all cronies at the caſtle? How does the venerable virgin Mrs. Buckram,

pretty

pretty Rachel Williams, and the reft of the fair nuns?

Simon. Name 'em not; you have not left your fellow. What is Rachel Williams? a baby.

Jenny. Well, but Mrs. Buckram—fhe is no baby.

Simon. No, o' my word; fhe is of the race of the Anakims.

Jenny. No matter for that, friend Simon; you'll marry Buckram.

Simon. No, no, that buckram fhall never ftick in my fkirts. Harapha of Gath wou'dn't marry her. I am no knight-errant to encounter giants.

Jenny. I fhou'd think fo; for if you were a true knight, you wou'd not fleep before you had fet free your lovely prifoner, Emily Fitzallan.

Simon. There's one a-coming will do that. Fair Emily will be a wife before you'll be a widow. Young Montrath is the man for her; he's expected every day with his uncle Sir Oliver. It is all agreed upon, and my lady's whole fortune will be fettled on Mifs Emily. There's a ftart for you—there's a fally from dependance to profperity; from wanting every thing to poffeffing all.

Jenny. And nothing left to Harry Algernon?

Simon. Yes, patience if he poffeffes it, and an ill-name whether he merits it or not.

Jenny. Well, I can't fee the juftice of all this.

Simon. Who can, where lawyer Earling is concerned? That puppy of an attorney lords it over the whole caftle; and now we are in the buftle of fetting out Mifs Emily in a ftile before Sir Oliver arrives. There are fine dreffes to be made, fine

apartments

apartments to be furniſhed, and freſh ſervants to be hir'd for the heireſs.

Jenny. Say you ſo ? freſh ſervants ? Are you full? If not, I can recommend you ſuch a lacquey—the very man of men—Jerry ſhall bring him to you.

Simon. Bring him yourſelf; lead him over in a white bridle, and let me judge of his points and his paces.

Jenny. You ſhall—my life for your's, Miſs Emily will be charm'd with him.

Simon. Adieu ! time flies when I am with you. Once more, adieu ! I ſhall expect you. I hope you are happy with your little doctor; but I muſt think you were much too fine a flower to be pluckt by an apothecary, and ſtuck into a gallipot. [*Exit.*

Jenny. He's off; you may come out of your hiding hole ; the coaſt is clear.

(Enter ALGERNON, *followed by* SCUD.)

Alg. Now, my fair advocate, what have you done for me ? Is there any hope ?

Jenny. Of the old lady's fortune, none ; your aunt has not left you a ſhilling.

Alg. I'm glad of it.

Scud. I wonder why.

Jenny. Miſs Emily is to have the whole.

Alg. I'm ſorry for it.

Scud. I wonder wherefore.

Alg. I'il tell you then. Had my aunt bequeath'd to me her fortune, ſhe wou'd have probably re-ſtricted me from marrying Emily; having given it to Emily, ſhe has doubtleſs tied her up from marrying me. Had ſhe done neither one nor the other, I have enough to maintain her, and the prize had been my own.

Jenny.

Jenny. And fo fhe fhall; I've a project for your meeting.

Alg. I doubt if I ought to feek it.

Scud. Very true; lay it afide altogether; it will bring a plaguy deal of mifchief upon me, and do no good to you.

Alg. Tell it me however.

Jenny. You'll comprehend it at once. There is a proper valet to be hir'd for the heirefs, fit to wait upon her perfon, and grace the back of her chair at table.

Alg. I can't do it; I am not equal to the tafk; I can't approach fo near, and yet refrain. When fhe fpoke to me, I fhou'd be loft; when fhe look'd on me, I fhou'd betray myfelf; and when I handed her the plate, I fhould prefent it on my knee.

Scud. Aye, then you wou'd be vollied out of the window, and I kick'd out of the doors. Now, filly Jenny, what's become of your project?

Alg. Hold there! tho' dangerous in the extreme it is not altogether defperate. If I cannot undertake the offices you defcribe, I may yet prefent myfelf as a candidate for her fervice; and in that character perhaps obtain an interview with my charmer. That hope is worth an effort.

Scud. It isn't worth a farthing, and will be pounds and pounds out of my way. Curfed fcrape, foolifh Jenny, curfed fcrape!

Alg. But where fhall I get a proper drefs to appear in?

Scud. No where; you can't appear at all.

Jenny. Fear nothing; I'll provide you with a drefs.

Scud.

Scud. Egad, fhe has a provifion for every thing.

Alg. Who but muft conquer that is armed by the fair ? There is a rafcal in the family, Earling by name, who has flanderoufly defam'd me ; I'll wring his ears from his head.

Scud. Take care ; Earling is an attorney, and if he has any ears you will pay for wringing them ; if he has none, you'll be puzzled to lay hold of them.

Alg. Come, Jerry, I fee what ftaggers you ; you are afraid of lofing the old lady's cuftom.

Scud. You are right ; I am. She takes phyfic, and you take pleafure.

Alg. Mark me ! I'll not promife you to fwallow as many medicines as fhe does ; but, come what will, I'll guarantee you againft all loffes incurr'd on my account ; fo fear nothing, but come on. Difcretion I can't boaft of, but in honour I will never be found wanting.

Scud. That's enough, that's enough ! Deal upon honour and I am with you. I love to do a good natur'd action when there's nothing to be loft by it.

[*Exeunt.*

SCENE *changes to an Apartment in Lady* CYPRESS's *Caftle.*

Lady CYPRESS, *Lawyer* EARLING.

Lady Cyp. Enter, enter, Mr. Earling : you come upon a wifh.

Earl. Ever prompt to approve myfelf your lady-fhip's moft devoted and moft abfolute humble fervant, upon a wifh I come, upon a word I vanifh.

Lady Cyp. I am fatisfied with your diligence ; you may fpare yourfelf the trouble of defcribing it.

Earl.

Earl. I am dumb.

Lady Cyp. Have you the memorandums about you, that I dictated ?

Earl. If my tears have not defac'd them. Believe me, gracious lady, when I faw my own name fet down to a bequeft fo munificent, I was cover'd with blufhes, I was choak'd with gratitude.

Lady Cyp. Out with it then, out with your name, if fuch is the effect, and write in Algernon's ; I warrant gratitude will not choak him.

Earl. Good, very good ! Your ladyfhip has the gift of rallying me in the moft pleafant way out of my metaphors. Choak is a figure fomewhat of the ftrongeft.

Lady Cyp. Why yes, and I fhou'd think you may venture upon the legacy, and rifque the effects of it ; fo copy out your paper when you pleafe.

Earl. I'll fet my clerks upon it out of hand.

Lady Cyp. You'll fet the world upon it when I'm out of it, for you have totally cafhier'd Harry Algernon, and he is the fon of my fifter.

Earl. And your fifter was the wife of his father, and his father was your unremitting perfecutor, who vex'd you with a fuit in chancery for ten long years, and ten might have been added to ten, had it not been that I—I fpeak modeftly of myfelf ; I am no egotift—I fpeak fimply of number one, and nobody elfe, for your barrifter was a cypher—

Lady Cyp. But a cypher put to number one adds no trifle to its value ; fo the upfhot is, you gain'd the fuit, and I paid the cofts—a victory little to be envied—and, after all, is it juft and equitable the fon fhould fuffer for the father's faults ?

Earl.

Earl. O jus et æquum ! as if he had not faults enough of his own to warrant your exclufion of him.

Lady Cyp. I have heard enough of his faults I confefs, if you are correct in defcribing them. If you have deceiv'd me—

Earl. I! I deceive you! I defame your nephew! I who have never fpoke of his offences but with regret and forrow ; never brought a ftory to your ears, but with the view of intercepting malice and foftening down impreffions ; I deceive you ! then where is truth and virtue ?

Lady Cyp. Both in fight, as I fhou'd hope—for Emily appears.

(EMILY FITZALLAN *enters.)*

Earl. I humbly take my leave. Mifs Emily, I'm your's—Humph ! not a word ! Your faithful friend to ferve you. Not a look ? Upftart ! I'll marry the old lady, and cut her out of every fhilling—I will.   [*Exit* EARLING.

Lady Cyp. Approach, my dear ! Come near me. I muft talk with you. Well ! You have been to fee the apartment I have newly furnifhed—and do you like it, Emily ?

Emily. 'Tis elegant in the extreme—'tis fumptuous.

Lady Cyp. 'Tis your's, my dear ; it is to grace my Emily that I have deck'd it out.

Emily. For me fuch finery ?

Lady Cyp. Child of my heart, for you. All I poffefs is your's.

Emily. I hope you will not tempt me to forget that I was poor and humble.

Lady

Lady Cyp. I hope not : nature has endow'd you with admirable qualities; profperity, I truft, will not pervert them. It does not quite come on you by furprize : you cou'd not well fuppofe I fhou'd adopt the fon of my moft unrelenting perfecutor.

Emily. I did not dare to reafon in that cafe.

Lady Cyp. But you muft know how worthlefs in himfelf, how undeferving of my favour is he, who, in refpect of confanguinity, is the only perfon that cou'd fuperfede you.

Emily. You fpeak of Mr. Algernon.

Lady Cyp. I do; I fpeak of him, whom no one fpeaks of but with reproach and fcorn.

Emily. I do confefs I've heard much evil fpeaking, but 'twas from one who fhou'd have more refpect for truth and decency than to traduce the nephew to the aunt.

Lady Cyp. What do you mean? Wou'd you defend a libertine ?

Emily. No, madam, I defend no libertine; but you will not be angry if I avow that I deteft a libeller. If he, who thus has poifon'd your opinion, knows not the character, the manners, habits, fentiments, connections, perhaps not even the outward form and feature of the man, whofe fame he mangles, can I be to blame if I implore you, for the love of juftice, to hear before you ftrike ?

Lady Cyp. What is this, Emily ? What is this warmth ?

Emily. Honeft, not prudent; out of time and place, but ftill fincere, tho' rafh.

Lady Cyp. You call on me to hear before I ftrike; I now demand if you that ftrike have heard ?

Do

Do you know Algernon ? Have you convers'd
with him ?

Emily. Madam, I have.

Lady Cyp. You have ! when; where ? he comes
not hither; never was admitted, never will be;
within thefe doors. Aftonifhing that you fhou'd
dare to tell me you have made acquaintance with
this profligate.

Emily. Hear my defence.——You gave me leave
to pafs a little time, for change of air after my late
confinement; at your Hill-farm. One evening I
had rambled about a mile from home, when upon
entering a little copfe; thro' which my footpath led,
judge of my horror; when a villain, fuch I muft
call him, furpriz'd me; feiz'd me, and in fpite of
cries, prayers and entreaties——

Lady Cyp. Merciful providence ! what do you
tell me ?

Emily. A dreadful tale I fhou'd have had to tell,
or died ere I cou'd tell it, had not heaven fent me
a refcue, a brave brave preferver, who with a foul
all fire, and motion quick as lightning; fprung on
the affailant, grafp'd him in his arms; and after a
contention, furious tho' fhort, hurl'd him to the
ground, breathlefs, and maim'd with bruifes.——
Which of thefe merits the name of *profligate ?* Not
he that fav'd me — It was Algernon.

Lady Cyp. Algernon do you fay ? My worthlefs
nephew Algernon ! Take care !

Emily. Renounce me if I tell you an untruth.

Lady Cyp. I'm all aftonifhment. Who was the
affailant ?

Emily. Madam, I know not. Your heroic
nephew

nephew bore me half dead and fainting to my houfe; 'twas not till then I knew him to be Algernon. He ftaid with me no longer than till the care of the good people had recovered me: the next morning I return'd to the caftle, fearing to remain any longer in fo folitary a place. Of Algernon, I faw no more. Now fuffer me to afk, is this the conduct of a profligate?

Lady Cyp. 'Tis a ftrange ftory.

Emily. 'Tis a true one, madam.

Lady Cyp. Why have you kept it to yourfelf thus long? You've been return'd two days.

Emily. Becaufe until this hour I have not feen your fpirits in a ftate to bear the flighteft agitation.

Lady Cyp. And do you think the agitation flight that I now fuffer? No, I fee your danger, Emily; I fee your weak credulity, and much I fear you'll find yourfelf the dupe of Algernon. What bufinefs cou'd he have at my Hill-farm?

Emily. Madam, your tenant's wife nurs'd Mr. Algernon.

Lady Cyp. She never fhou'd have nurs'd you, Emily, or harbour'd you one moment, had I known it.

Emily. That's hard; but I muft fuffer and be filent.

Lady Cyp. Be filent then, and go to your chamber; there you may meditate on what you have been, and call to mind, with timely recollection, what you may be again.

END OF ACT I.

ACT II.

Caſtle Hall.—Simon Single, *Farmer* Gawdry, *and his Son* Isaac.

Simon. MASTER Gawdry, Maſter Gawdry, have I not ſaid the word, and will not the word that I have ſaid ſerve and ſuffice to put thee out of doubt, that Iſaac thy ſon, thy ſon Iſaac, will not do?

Gawd. I pray you now, Maſter Simon Single, be kind-hearted, and conſider of it. I ſhou'd be main proud to have him in my lady's livery; he's a docile lad, and can turn his hand, as I may ſay, to any thing.

Simon. Let him turn it to the plough; he's a bumpkin: let him drive the team and dung the land; he's born to it: let him ring the hogs, and tend the ſtye, and toil in the drudgery of his vocation. Nature never faſhion'd him to be the lacquey of a lady—You are anſwer'd, farmer Gawdry.

Gawd. Aye, Maſter, I am anſwer'd, but I am not heard. I hann'a told you half the things my boy can do.

Simon. What can he do? Unfold!

Gawd. A power—Speak for yourſelf, Iſaac; tell the gentleman what you can do.

Iſaac. A'looks ſo grave, a'daunts me.

Gawd. What ſhou'd daunt thee, boy? Don't hang thy head, but up, and tell him boldly what can'ſt do.

Iſaac

Isaac. I wull, father, I wull.—I can fing pfalms, fhoot flying, worm the puppies, cut capons, climb the rookeries, and make gins for polecats.

Simon. Wonderful! and can't you eat and drink, and fleep and fnore abundantly? Can't you wench when you have an opportunity, fwear now and then upon occafion, and lie a little when it ferves your purpofe?

Isaac. Yes, yes, I know fomething of all thefe matters.

Gawd. I told you he was fit to wait upon any lady in the land.

Simon. Upon any lady but the lady Cyprefs he is welcome; upon her he may wait long enough before he gets any other anfwer than I've given you. *Dictum eft*—Good morning to you.

Gawd. Good morning to me indeed! How long, I trow, have you been this great man, to carry yourfelf in your geers fo ftately? I can call to mind the day when you came into this family as mere a bumpkin as you think my boy to be.

Simon. Keep your temper, neighbour Gawdry, keep your temper; mount your fteed, amble homewards, vifit your *oves* and your *boves*, comfort your good dame, and prefent my humble fervice to her.

Gawd. I won't comfort her; I won't prefent your humble fervice to her; I don't find you are fo willing to do her any fervice, and as for humble, it don't belong to you—but mark my words—time is at hand—county election's coming on—afk me for a plumper then, do; afk me, I fay, for a plumper

C —and

—and mind where I'll direct you to look for it.
Come along, Ifaac, come along!

[Exeunt GAWDRY *and* ISAAC.

Simon. We men in power, when we have a place to
give away, make nine enemies to one friend, and 'tis
nine to one if that friend don't turn an enemy
before he is well warm in his office.—Ah, Doctor,
is it you?

SCUD *and* SIMON SINGLE.

Scud. Your fervant, your fervant! I have brought
you the young man Jenny recommended.

Simon. Have you fo, have you fo? Where did
you fall in with him?

Scud. Crofs'd upon him by mere chance—clever
fellow—wants a place—think he'll fuit Mifs Emily—
no objection, dare fay, on his part—won't haggle
for wages—will you fee him?

Simon. Hold a moment.—Has he got a character?

Scud. Two—a good one and a bad one; but
the good one is what he wou'd prefer being known
by.

Simon. I give him credit for that. What name
does he bear?

Scud. Henry, alias Harry—you may take your
choice.

Simon. He has two of them, it feems; very good!
What befides?

Scud. Scudamore.

Simon. A branch of the Scuds we'll fuppofe;
but we'll fee him.—Where does he come from?

Scud. T'other fide of the country—better let
him

him anfwer queſtions for himſelf—come in, young
man; preſent yourſelf to Mr. Simon Single, the
reſpectable major domo of this illuſtrious family.

ALGERNON *enters.*

Simon. So, ſo! what's here? This is no drudge for
all work and all weathers; this is a thing for Sun-
days and for holidays! as clean a peg to hang a
livery on as heart cou'd wiſh.—Well, Henry Scudamore, you're for a place, and, I conclude, one where
there's leaſt to do will pleaſe you moſt; you are
not us'd to labour.

Alg. I am not.

Simon. Nor ever mean to be, I dare believe.

Scud. Oh fie! you'll put him down; he's modeſt
to a fault.

Simon. If that's his only fault, we'll overlook it.
What can you do?

Alg. My beſt to pleaſe my miſtreſs, and ſome-
thing, I ſhould hope, to gain your favour.

Simon. Egad, you've found the way to that already; I like your anſwer much; I like your manners,
countenance, deportment; and I am no mean judge,
altho' I ſay it.

Alg. Sir, you have all the right in life to ſay it;
for if none elſe will give us a good word, we muſt
e'en praiſe ourſelves.

Simon. A ſharp wit, let me tell you.—Harkee,
Henry, your name I know; the place from whence
you come I do not know; your qualifications remain to be prov'd, and your character I dare ſay,
if it is of your own giving, will be an excellent good
one.

C 2

Alg.

Alg. With your leave I ſhou'd prefer to ſpeak upon all theſe points with the lady I aſpire to ſerve.

Simon. *Aſpire to ſerve!* Sir, your moſt obedient humble ſervant.—I ſhall *aſpire* to aſk you no further queſtions, but turn you over for examination to the lady of the houſe herſelf.

Alg. Is this the lady of the houſe now approaching?

Mrs. DOROTHY BUCKRAM *enters.*

Simon. Of the lower houſe ſhe is the lady. Make your beſt bow to Mrs. Dorothy Buckram, but don't be too aſpiring; if you offer to ſalute her you are a loft man; that bleſſing don't fall to my lot above once in a twelvemonth, and ſome would not aſpire even to that.

Dor. What is this ribaldry that you are talking? and who is this young man?

Simon. A youth of promiſe; a candidate for ſervice; one that aſpires to the ſupreme delight of carrying clogs and combing lap-dogs for the lady heireſs.

Dor. What is his name.

Simon. Henry.

Dor. A gentle name, ſoothing and ſoft, I much approve of Henry: I've ever had a prejudice for Henry.

Simon. Simon is ſweeter.

Scud. Jerry is more briſk.

Simon. Sweet Simon—ſimple Simon—why 'ts muſic—it is a lute.

Scud. But Jerry founded in F ſharp's a trumpet.

Dor. Yes, truly, in the ears of a hen-peck'd huſband when his partlet cackles.—But can't this youngſter ſpeak? Henry ſhou'd ſpeak like Henry; let us hear you. Were I the miſtreſs you aſpir'd to ſerve, what wou'd you ſay to me?

Alg.

Alg. Silence becomes a fervant; 'tis a virtue; but if I were your equal and your lover.—

Dor. Ah, then what wou'd you fay?

Alg. Then if you ftood all tempting as you are, full in my fight, and cheer'd your happy fwain with fmiles fo lovely, languifh fo alluring.—

Dor. What wou'd you do?

Alg. I'd fnatch you to my heart, prefs you, carefs you, fmother you with fondnefs.—

Dor. And fo you will; let go, or I'll fcream out.

Simon. Bravo; you'll do—A very good rehearfal.

Scud. A very villanous one, if my Jenny has had a part in it.

Simon. I give you joy, young man; your fortune's made.

Dor. I wonder who has taught him this affurance.

Scud. Oh madam, he's a pupil of my Jenny's; I've nothing to do with him.

Simon. Come, come, there's no offence; t'was a fair challenge, and no true Englifhman wou'd have refus'd it.—Courage, my lad! you'll never want a fervice. Let us adjourn. [*Exeunt.*

(*Lady* CYPRESS *and Lawyer* EARLING.)

Lady Cyp. Well, now you've heard the ftory, what do you fay to it?

Earl. Nothing.

Lady Cyp. What, nothing? then you don't believe it.

Earl. Pardon me, madam; I believe it happened juft as Mifs Emily relates it to you; I do believe there was a man fet on to frighten her, and that he took a drubbing from her hero, for which I alfo perfectly believe he was well paid.

Lady Cyp.

Lady Cyp. Why fhou'd you not fuppofe it might be real? there are fuch drunken fellows up and down.

Earl. But fober men will not be taken in by fuch ftale tricks. You meet the fame, or fomething very like it, in every paltry novel that you read. The man's efcap'd; you'll never hear of him; his bargain was not made to go to prifon.

Lady Cyp. I fee it now; I fee thro' the contrivance.

Earl. Yes, madam, and you may alfo fee which way your property will go, if ever Mifs has the difpofal of it.

Lady Cyp. I'll never fign thofe deeds in her behalf till fhe confents to marry as I'd have her. Indeed, indeed, you have fav'd me, my good Sir, from a moft rafh and inconfiderate meafure.

Earl. Now is the time; I'll feize the happy moment.—My ever honour'd lady, I but live to fave and ferve you; my whole life has been devoted to your happinefs; the founder of your fortune, I have fought your battles manfully, and ftood a fiege as long as that of Troy in your defence; aye, and wou'd die in it if need requir'd.

Lady Cyp. There is no need—I know your fervices, and at my death you'll find I have not underrated them.

Earl. She melts—I'll ftrike.—Not at your death, dear lady, (may that be far, far off!) but with your life reward me.—Hah! that tells fhe yields to the impreffion.—

Lady Cyp. How with my life? You have my good opinion; you have my friendfhip; what more can I do for you?

Earl.

Earl. Think of me only as I think of you. Why shou'd a thanklefs girl engrofs your fortune? Ufe it; employ it; many happy days are yet in ftore for you. When the Lord Cyprefs married you he was your fenior by a pretty many years more than your ladyfhip is mine.

Lady Cyp. Your inference from that?

Earl. I dare not quite reveal it. I wou'd wifh your ladyfhip to take it to your thoughts. A hint, a word, a look, fo it were kind, wou'd greatly help me to declare it to you.

Lady Cyp. We'll talk no more at prefent, if you pleafe; you will remember you're my agent, Sir; and I will not forget your fervices.—Good day to you.

Earl. May every day and every hour be happy as I cou'd wifh them, and you will be bleft.—'Twill do—her pride is dropping from the perch—fhe totters; I fhall catch her.   [*Exit.*

SIMON SINGLE *enters.*

Lady Cyp. How now, Simon! have you found a proper lad amongft the tenants fons to ferve Mifs Emily?

Simon. Of them not one, fo help me, honor'd lady—I cannot recommend them; they are boors, clowns, clodpates.

Lady Cyp. What is to be done?

Simon. There is a youth attending—Doctor Scud fpeaks in his favour.

Lady Cyp. Scud's a babbler.—What do you fay?

Simon. He is above the level of thefe indigenous fmock-frocks and hobnails. I fhou'd advife your ladyfhip to fee him.

Lady

Lady Cyp. By all means; let him enter.

Simon. Henry, you are permitted to approach; the Lady Cyprefs deigns to look upon you—make your obeifance!

ALGERNON *enters.*

Lady Cyp. So! this is the young man—Henry you call him; what other name belongs to him?

Simon. Scudamore, an pleafe you; fo he gives in himfelf.

Lady Cyp. No vulgar name—and, fo far as appearances befpeak, no vulgar perfon. Well, Henry Scudamore, you want a place.

Alg. I wifh to ferve your ladyfhip.

Lady Cyp. Have you been in fervice?

Alg. Never.

Lady Cyp. So I fhou'd guefs. What leads you now to feek it?

Alg. The ambition of belonging to your ladyfhip; but I wou'd anfwer more directly, might I prefume.—

Lady Cyp. I underftand you. Simon, leave the room.   [*Exit* SIMON.
You feem embarrafs'd. Was it not your wifh to fpeak to me in private?

Alg. Madam, it was.

Lady Cyp. And what have you to impart, that one, who poffibly may be your fellow fervant, might not be privy to?

Alg. Madam, I am a gentleman by birth; that being known amongft my fellow fervants might chance to raife an evil mind againft me, and make my humble ftation painful to me; your candour will not think the worfe of me becaufe I am unfortunate.

Lady

Lady Cyp. No, not the worfe in charity of thought, but I cannot employ you in my fervice. No gentleman muft wait upon that lady, to whom I elfe perhaps had deftin'd you. – No gentleman at leaft of your appearance.

Alg. I'm forry for it—but it is my fate to be judg'd by appearances, and condemn'd by reports.

Lady Cyp. If you have fallen into this decay by mere misfortune, or injurious treatment, I can pity you ; nay, Henry Scudamore, if that's your name, and if I knew your ftory (which at prefent I have not time to hear) I cou'd do more—I cou'd (and fomething whifpers me I wou'd) confider your neceffities, and help you.

Alg. I am the victim, madam, of a villain. My ftory is foon told, for it is founded on a fimple fact, which I can make appear to full conviction, if you will condefcend to give me hearing, and fuffer me to ftate fuch evidence, as cannot be oppos'd by my defamer.

Lady Cyp. I know not what to fay to that, young man ; I have no ftrength to fpare for other's burthens, and am already loaded with my own, even to the breaking down of my weak frame. If 'tis a cafe of pity, I've a hand that's open to your wants without enquiry ; if it is matter of grievance and redrefs, I wou'd recommend you to ftate it to my lawyer, Mr. Earling, and he fhall fee you righted.

Alg. I humbly thank you ; I will ftate it to him, and truft the goodnefs of your heart will fee me righted.

Lady Cyp. Ah ! I've no heart, no health, no nerves to hear you. You muft excufe me, Henry Scudamore.

Scudamore. I dare not undertake to arbitrate; but wait Sir Oliver Montrath's arrival, and he shall hear you; he's a noble gentleman.

Alg. Where shall I wait the whilst?

Lady Cyp. Where? Let me see—yes, you may stay this night here in the castle. My old servant, Simon, will entertain you at the second table. Does that content you?

Alg. I were most unthankful if it did not.

Lady Cyp. Follow me then, and I will give my orders.   [*Exeunt.*

EMILY's *Apartment.*

EMILY FITZALLAN, RACHEL WILLIAMS.

Emily. Rachel!

Rachel. Madam! what are your commands?

Emily. Don't answer me in that stile. I have so long been a dependant, and liv'd in such familiarity with you, my good Rachel, in particular, that, tho' you are my servant, I don't wish you to use a language to me so submissive.

Rachel. Whatever language you wou'd have me use, so it will but convey the same respect, I will endeavour to conform to it.

Emily. I wou'd fain keep upon such terms with fortune, that I may fall back to my former poverty without a pang; therefore, if ever you perceive me giddy with prosperity, recal my recollection to the low situation I emerg'd from, and do it honestly, my girl; don't spare me.

Rachel. You'll want no monitor to warn you against pride, and yet, as you require sincerity, there is one warning I conceive is needful just at this crisis.

Emily. State it without reserve.

Rachel.

Rachel. Are you not now in danger of incurring your patroness's moſt ſevere diſpleaſure ?

Emily. Perhaps I am ; but be explicit with me.

Rachel. Your champion Algernon, has he not left a thorn in that ſoft heart?

Emily. If you call gratitude a thorn, he has.

Rachel. Are you quite ſure 'tis only gratitude ? May it not ſoon be love ? Nay, give me leave—— is it not love already ?

Emily. Well, if it is, how can I ſtrive againſt it ?

Rachel. Prudence will tell you how.

Emily. Prudence will tell me an old goſſip's tale, but who, that is in love, will hear her out ?

Rachel. Are you aware how fatal it will be to all your expectations, if my lady diſcovers your attachment ?

Emily. Are you aware how natural it is to love the man who ſaves you from deſtruction ? My lady gives me riches, Algernon reſcues my life and honour ; I was loſt but for his courage ; I am only poor without her bounty ; and if ſhe demands that I ſhou'd ſacrifice my heart's affections, ſhe makes conditions that I cannot grant, nor wou'd her fortune bribe me to the attempt.

Rachel. Do you know Mr. Algernon's character?

Emily. Does he that blackens it ? What does my lady know but what that lawyer inſtils into her ear ? Infamous man ! And why does he defame him ? why, but becauſe he may retain his power in the eſtate, and garbel it at pleaſure ? Beſides, he has an ample legacy ; believe me, I hold it a diſgrace to read my name in the ſame page with his ; nor wou'd I be his partner in the crime of plundering

4   Algernon,

Algernon, but that I live in hopes the time will come when I may render back the unlawful fpoil.

Rachel. Then temporize the whilft, my deareft lady, or that time never will be your's.

Emily. 'Tis right; you counfel well; and now I will confide a fecret to you : I have warn'd Algernon who is his enemy, and what bafe ftories have been forg'd againft him,—Ah! who is this? 'Tis he, 'tis he himfelf!

Algernon enters.

Alg. Hufh! not fo loud.

Emily. Your name was on my lips. How came you here? How did you gain admiffion, and what have you in view by this difguife? You may difclofe ; this friendly girl is fecret.

Alg. Then let her ftay; I wou'd not be furpriz'd in private with you, I am here by fufferance of Lady Cyprefs; I have feen my aunt for the firft time, convers'd with her, and lodg'd a plea for further hearing when her friend, Sir Oliver Montrath, fhall be at leifure: one of his fervants is already come; he may be foon expected.

Emily. And his nephew, does he accompany him?

Alg. I did not afk that queftion of the fervant, but if you wifh it I will make the enquiry.

Emily. No, let it pafs. I know your aunt expects him.—Hark, Rachel, fomebody is at the door —fee who it is.

Rachel. Madam, there's nobody, nor any found that I can hear.

Emily. Stand where you are and liften !—What is the meaning of this drefs you wear?

Alg. I put it on to counterfeit a fervant, or, I fhou'd rather fay, to afk for fervice—Will you not

6

try

try me, Emily? don't take my character from that attorney; I'll serve you honestly.

Emily. You serve! you're jesting.

Alg. Am I not your servant? I am your faithful servant.

Emily. My heroic preserver—that is your rightful character, and by that title you have a claim upon my gratitude, which only can expire with life—and now inform me what you have in view by this adventure.

Alg. I am not so romantic as to think I can maintain my post longer than till to-morrow, to which time I have a furlough by authority; if fortune stands my friend I may effect something within that period; but even now am I not supremely blest to see you, hear you, and behold that face, that was of late so pale and wan with terror, restor'd to all the lustre of its charms?

Emily. That face, assure yourself, will never be turn'd from you to league with those who seek to rob you of your fame and fortune.

Alg. I am not robb'd of what enriches you.

Emily. The heart, that swells with indignation against all that wrong you, had but for you been cold and motionless.—

Alg. Oh Emily, forbear.

Emily. This and no more—I never will be made the slave of interest or dupe of slander. My confidence in you cannot be shaken, my obligations cannot be computed. The life that I possess is of your giving—What can I say but that I live for you?—Now leave me, Henry; not a word, but leave me.

END OF ACT II.

A C T III.

Lady Cypress *and Servant.*

LADY CYPRESS.

HARK! 'tis the porter's bell—run to the hall, and tell me if Sir Oliver's arriv'd.

Serv. Madam, he's here: Sir Oliver is prefent.

Sir OLIVER MONTRATH *enters.*

Lady Cyp. Welcome, moft welcome! May I truft my fenfes? This is above hope that you and I fhould live to meet again.

Sir Oliv. My ever dear, my ever honour'd lady!

Lady Cyp. Time has gone lightly over you, my friend! You, that have travers'd fea and land, are whole; I, that have tempted neither, am become a fhatter'd wreck on fhore.

Sir Oliv. Not fo, not altogether fo, thank heaven! Time is a furly gueft, whofe courtefy does not improve by long acquaintance with us; but we'll not rail at him fince he permits us once more to meet.—And here's the fame old caftle ftill unfpoilt by modern foppery; aye, and the fame old grand fires firm in their frames with not one wrinkle more than when I parted from them years ago.

Lady Cyp. Aye, years indeed—but you have fill'd them up with glory; your's has been a life of themes for future hiftory, a field of laurels to adorn your tomb—mine has been tame and fimple vegetation.

Sir Oliv. I have liv'd a foldier's life; but, heaven be

be thank'd, I've plunder'd no nabob, ftript no rajah of his pearls and pagodas, nor have I any blood upon my fword, but what a foldier's honour may avow—but you have here a relict of my gallant comrade major Antony ⬥zallan. He was wounded by my fide, carried off the field, and died in my arms. With his laft breath he bequeath'd ('twas all he had to beftow) a bleffing to his daughter, and charg'd me, if I liv'd to come to England, to thank you for your charity, and be a friend to her.

Lady Cyp. I truft you'll find her worthy of your friendfhip.

Sir Oliv. Is fhe good, is fhe amiable? Has fhe her father's principles, her mother's purity?

Lady Cyp. See her and judge; fhe's naturally fincere—but where's your nephew? where is Mr. Lionel?—I reckon'd with much pleafure upon feeing him.

Sir Oliv. Ah, my good lady, there I am unfortunate. I had built upon the hopes of prefenting him to you; but it cannot be at prefent. Poor Lionel is indifpos'd, and muft bear his difappointment with what philofophy he can.

Lady Cyp. The difappointment is reciprocal—a little time I hope will bring him to us.

Sir Oliv. I wifh it may—but look! who comes—

Lady Cypr. This is my orphan charge—This is our Emily.

EMILY FITZALLAN *enters.*
Sir Oliv. The very image of her lovely mother.

Lady Cyp. My dear, this is Sir Oliver Montrath, mine and your father's friend; as fuch you'll honour him.

Sir

Sir Oliv. As fuch I claim the privilege to embrace and prefs her to my heart. My child, my charge, devolv'd upon me by a father's legacy, when breathing out his gallant foul in prayers and bleffings for his Emily.

Emily. Oh fir, was you, was you befide him at that dreadful moment?

Sir Oliv. I was, my child! thefe arms fupported him, cover'd with wounds, and crown'd with victory—alas! how dearly purchas'd.

Emily. Then let his laft commands be ever facred; if you have any fuch in charge to give me, impart them, I conjure you.

Sir Oliv. I have none but bleffings to impart. In fortune's gifts the hero had no fhare, in virtue's he abounded. In the care of this your generous benefactrefs he had left you; to that and heaven's protection he bequeath'd you.

Emily. I am content; and what before I ow'd in gratitude to this beneficent and noble lady, I now will pay with filial obedience and duty fuper-added. Suffer me, deareft madam, from this moment to call myfelf your daughter.

Lady Cyp. As fuch I have adopted you; remember now, my child, the duty you have taken on yourfelf, the authority you have confign'd to me. All rights parental center now in me; your happinefs, your credit, your eftablifhment, are trufts for which I am refponfible.—You have no other tafk but to obey.

Emily. Obedience, madam, has its limitations; bu⁺ fuch as I would render to my father I'll pay to you. Have I your leave to withdraw?

Lady

Lady Cyp. You may, my dear; your spirits seem to need it.—Go and compose yourself.

[*Exit* EMILY.

Sir Oliv. Exquisite creature! I'm enchanted with her. By heaven! 'twould be the heighth of my ambition, the object I have most at heart in life, to see my Lionel—Oh that I cou'd!—here kneeling at her feet.—Born of such parents, train'd by such instructions, and grac'd with charms so lovely, Emily, without a fortune, is a match for princes.

Lady Cyp. If such is your disinterested wish (and greater happiness I could not pray for) I trust my fortune thrown into her scale will not make her appear less worthy of your nephew, or cause you to retract your good opinion.

Sir Oliv. No, surely; but I doubt if I should wish your fortune to go out of the right channel even to Emily. We that have never married should regard our nephews as our sons.

Lady Cyp. But does affinity impose on me an obligation to bestow my property on one that merits nothing, to the wrong of her that merits all?

Sir Oliv. Is that the character of Algernon? Is he so undeserving?

Lady Cyp. Ah there, my friend, there is my terror; the destiny I dread; the man of all men living the most dangerous to my peace is Algernon.

Sir Oliv. Indeed!

Lady Cyp. Preserve my Emily from him—save her from Algernon!

Sir Oliv. Is Algernon then born to be a curse to both of us?

D

Lady

Lady Cyp. Explain yourſelf.

Sir Oliv. He is your nephew, therefore I was ſilent ; but if he's dangerous to your peace of mind, to mine he's fatal—in one word, the wound of which my hapleſs Lionel now languiſhes was given by the hand of Algernon.

Lady Cyp. Horrible wretch !—his murderer.—

Sir Oliv. I ſay not that; for modern courteſy gives not that name to duelliſts, and honour ſanctifies their bloody deeds.

Lady Cyp. Away with all ſuch honour ! Truth diſavows it, nature revolts from it, religion denounces it—Oh! he is born to be my ſhame and torment.

Sir Oliv. Be patient for a while; ſuſpend your judgment.

Lady Cyp. No, I regard a duelliſt with horror; I hold him as an agent of the enemy of mankind, ſent to diſturb ſociety, and rend the parent's and the widow's hearts aſunder : one action, one only action, and that a doubtful one, had met my ear in favour of that wretch whom I call nephew, and henceforth even that one I totally diſcredit, and renounce him.

Sir Oliv. Hold, I conjure you. In the midſt of wrath let us remember juſtice. I, like you, abhor a duelliſt profeſt; yet I am taught by long experience how to make allowances for younger ſpirits, and warmer paſſions, that will not ſubmit to meet the world's contempt, and ſcorn its prejudices.

Lady Cyp. Away! you talk this language by profeſſion; reaſon declares againſt it.

Sir Oliv. Reaſon demands that we ſhould pauſe

in

in judgment. When two men draw their fwords upon each other, reafon will tell us one muft be to blame; but ere we fix the blame upon that one, juftice decrees that we fhould hear them both.

Lady Cyp. What fays your nephew? He will fpeak the truth.

Sir Oliv. I fhould expect he would; yet I'll not wholly truft to any man's report againft another in his own caufe; and in this fentiment my nephew honourably coincides, for he declines all anfwer to my queftions, and will ftate nothing to affect or criminate his antagonift—Hah! who is this?

ALGERNON *enters.*

Lady Cyp. Go, go! I did not fend for you.

Alg. I know it; but I wifh to fpeak in private with Sir Oliver Montrath.

Sir Oliv. With me? Who is this man? I do not know him. Is he one of your ladyfhip's domeftics?

Lady Cyp. No; he made offer of his fervices, but upon talking with him I perceiv'd he had a lift of grievances to ftate, and not being then at leifure, I believe I told him he might wait your coming, and make his fuit to you.

Sir Oliv. And fo he may—his looks plead in his caufe. Is it your wifh to fpeak with me, young man?

Alg. It is.

Sir Oliv. Alone?

Alg. Alone, if you'll permit it.

Sir Oliv. Freely; and when I can command my time, it fhall be your's. I'll call for you.

Alg.

Alg. I fhall attend your fummons.

[*Exit* ALGERNON.

Sir Oliv. I'm curious what this man can have to tell me. Do you conjecture?

Lady Cyp. There is a myftery about him. He fays he is a gentleman by birth, and fo far I believe him. Of what he had to tell befides I wav'd the hearing, but offer'd him relief: that did not feem his object, nor was it mine to take a gentleman into my fervice. But you will know the whole—fhall we adjourn and fee what is become of Emily?

Sir Oliv. With all my heart; and hope the mournful fubject of our laft interview may be no more reviv'd.   [*Exeunt.*

SCENE *changes.*

LAWYER EARLING *meeting* ALGERNON.

Earl. So! whence come you? who are you? what's your bufinefs?

Alg. Sir, I don't know you.

Earl. Not know me? that's much. You muft be new indeed.

Alg. Are you that worthy gentleman Mr. Earling?

Earl. I am the very perfon.

Alg. Heaven reward you! Your fame is founded forth thro' all the county.

Earl. Are you not hir'd to wait on Mifs Fitzallan?

Alg. No, Sir, my character don't feem to recommend me to the Lady Cyprefs. If you wou'd fpeak for me 'twou'd make my fortune.

Earl. How can I fpeak for you, whom I don't know?   *Alg.*

Alg. 'Twou'd be as eafy as to fpeak againſt me.

Earl. But I do neither ; I have no concern with you or with your character.

Alg. Indeed ! they told me you was famous for it.

Earl. For what is it I'm famous ?

Alg. For fpeaking about characters you've no concern with ; therefore I pray you, fir, take, mine in hand, and do me juſtice. I fuſpect fome villain has cruelly defam'd me.—Doesn't an action lie for that at law ?

Earl. Go ! you're a fool ; begone !

Alg. I am a fool to aſk a knave for juſtice.

[*Exit.*

Earl. Knave ! do you call me knave ? I'll trounce you, firrah ! I'll blow you to the moon, audacious beggar ! Ah, maſter Doctor, do you know that raſcal ?

SCUD *enters.*

Scud. I know feveral raſcals, but which of them do you mean ?

Earl. That impudent new comer, that mad fellow, that dares to infult me in my lady's houfe.— Call me a knave indeed, and to my face—did you ever hear fuch infolence ?

Scud. Never, never : If he had only faid it behind your back, why 'twere but quid for quo ; it would have pafs'd ; but to your face—Oh monſtrous !

Earl. I'll fet him in the ſtocks ; I'll have his ears nailed to the whipping poſt.

Scud. No, don't do that ; if whipping-poſts had ears, they'd hear the cries of thofe that are tied to them, and pity them.

Earl. Pooh ! you're as great a fool as he me-

D 3   thinks :

thinks: I've done with you.—Look to yourfelf, Sir Gallipot, your reign will not be long on this ground, take my word for it.   [*Exit.*

Scud. There, there, there! I'm blown up, oufted, all is over with me. Thought to have had my lady's cuftom till her death—perceive now fhe will be one of the few patients that out live my prefcriptions.— Oh fine work, fine work!

ALGERNON *enters.*

Alg. How now, friend Scud; what ails you?

Scud. Friend! call me fool. I'm ruin'd by my friendfhip. You've play'd the devil's dance with that damn'd lawyer, and fet him whip and fpur upon my back.

Alg. Why that's his proper place: back-biting is his trade.

Scud. And what's my trade, do you think? where fhall I drive it? my gallipots may grow into the fhelves for everlafting, if I'm to be made the cat's-paw of your fchemes and foolifh Jenny's—but I'll go tell my lady all about you.

Alg. No, no, you'll not do that, my little Scud.

Scud. I'll tell you what I won't do—lofe my cuftomer.

Alg. Aye, but confider what an ornament your ears are to your head, and you'll lofe them incontinently if you betray me.

Scud. My ears indeed! look to your own; the lawyer has fworn to nail them to the whipping poft. I've got a wig, fo have not you, my mafter. Befides, I'm not quite certain but my lady's cuftom will be the greater lofs.—She takes a world of phyfic.

SIMON

Simon Single *enters.*

Simon. Who talks of phyfic? I've the beft of medicines—a cafe of old canary, which my lady has order'd us to tap, and drink a welcome to our noble gueft, Sir Oliver Montrath.—I've put my lips to it : 'tis fupernaculum.

Scud. I fee you have; I fee 'tis fupernaculum, for fome of it has got under your wig already.

Simon. My wig; no, no, Dame Dorothy fet that awry with a kind cuff o'the ear.

Scud. You put your lips to her too, it fhould feem.

Simon. Perhaps I did, but that's all buckram, Doctor. Ah Henry, give me your hand. Stand faft, my gallant hearts; lo, where fhe comes again, a portly fail right on upon our convoy. My life upon't, fhe's bound to the Canaries.

Mrs. Dorothy *enters,*

Dor. Oh thou rafh youth, thou haft undone thy-felf. Earling has vow'd thy ruin.

Scud. He has vow'd my ruin too, and that is one of the few vows that he will keep religioufly.

Dor. Ah, he's a carnal man; he'll fwallow up this caftle and it's fortunes.

Simon. I hope the turrets of it will ftick by the way, and choak him. He fha'n't fwallow the canary in it however; we'll be beforehand with him at that fport.

Scud. I would I had the cooking of one dofe for him. I wifh he'd fwallow that. It fhou'd be a fettler.

Dor. What has he done by Harry Algernon? There's malice for you; there's a batch of mifchief;

blafted

blaſted his character, garbled his fortune, and turn'd my lady's heart to ſtone againſt him.

Simon. Flint, iron, adamant—I told her ſo—Madam, ſaid I, the gentleman is wrong'd; the neighbours, where he lives, all give him a good word, the gentry love him, his father doats on him, the poor adore him : there is but one bad character 'twixt him and your attorney—Judge you, ſaid I, which party it belongs to.

Alg. Did you ſay this ?

Simon. I did.

Alg. Then you're an honeſt fellow.

Simon. I know that well enough.   Yes, I did ſay it.

Scud. How did ſhe take it ?

Simon. As ſhe takes your phyſic—gulp'd and made wry faces; but it went down.

Scud. I hope 'twill ſtay by her.

Simon. I hope it will, and when we've drank confuſion to attornies, I'll deal her out another doſe a little ſtronger.   Damn it !—no, hold, I will not ſwear—I'll do it coolly—come, we'll call a council in the Canaries.

Scud. Agreed; I'll drink myſelf into a little courage, and have a word with the old laſs myſelf.

Simon. Come on, my hearts ! Henry, conduct the lady.   You may ſolicit her fair hand in ſafety. Jerry and I have wigs.   [*Exeunt,*

SCENE *changes.*

Lady CYPRESS, EMILY, *Sir* OLIVER MONTRATH, EARLING,

Lady Cyp. Now, Emily, you ſee what miſery that wicked man has brought upon us all.

- 3   *Emily,*

Emily. I'm forry for Sir Oliver's misfortune.

Lady Cyp. I hope you have alfo pity for the fufferer.

Emily. I truft I have for all that merit it.

Earl. I'm fure Mifs Emily will not attempt to extenuate the guilt of fuch an action.

Emily. You may be fure I never will defend a guilty perfon, knowing him for fuch; be you as careful how you criminate an abfent man, till you have proofs againft him. [*To Sir* OLIVER.] Sir, you are filent; I fhould wifh to know if you have any thing to urge againft him.

Sir Oliv. Nothing, my dear, I'm liftening with attention, and therefore filent. I fhould be forry were you lefs unwilling to give up your opinion of a man who render'd you fuch fervice.

Lady Cyp. What fervice? Earling, you have heard the ftory; let us hear what you have to fay upon it.

Earl. If Mifs Fitzallan will fuffer me to put a fimple queftion to her.

Emily. By all means; put your queftion.

Earl. When Mr. Algernon, by happy chance, came in fo opportunely to her refcue, can Mifs Fitzallan fay what brought him thither fo far from his own home?

Emily. I never afk'd what caus'd him to be there, nor did he tell me.

Earl. We'll call it then a very happy chance without a caufe, or a moft fortunate prefentiment that fomewhere in that grove there would be found a damfel in the power of fome vile ruffian, whom he was doom'd to refcue. Some people might fuppofe

this

this a collusion, but Miss Fitzallan can remove all
doubts by telling us who was the villain that offer'd
her that violence.

Sir Oliv. Can you do this, my Emily ?

Emily. I cannot.

Earl. Did Mr. Algernon know who he was ?

Emily. I do not think he did.

Earl. Did he secure his person ?

Emily. No ; his care was wholly turn'd to me ;
the man he left upon the ground, and, as it seem'd,
disabled.

Earl. I have done : I leave it to the court to judge.

Lady Cyp. A barefac'd trick. It is too pal-
pable.

Sir Oliv. Who can say that ?—Let Mr. Algernon
speak for himself.

Eatl. Speak!

Sir Oliv. Aye, you have spoke, and should not
he ? That's justice, is it not ?

Earl. Did you always find it so where you have
been, Sir Oliver ?

Sir Oliv. Whether I found it so or not, I felt it.

Emily. Now, Mr. Earling, you may put those
questions, you've press'd on me, to Mr. Algernon,
Perhaps he'll answer them.

Lady Cyp. Emily, Emily, you forget yourself.

Emily. Madam, I should, if I forbore to speak,
when charges such as these are urg'd against an
absent, therefore a defenceless, man. You have not
allow'd him to approach you, madam ; this gentleman, equally unknown to him, prejudges him at
once ; he is ingenious to find out bad motives for
good actions ; there's not a virtue in the human
heart

heart but may be metamorphos'd by such cunning into a vice. Sir Oliver has said, and said it in the language of a hero—*Let Mr. Algernon speak for himself.*

Sir Oliv. And I repeat those words.—Let him be heard!—However circumstances bear against him, and wretched tho' he has made me, still I hold it matter of conscience never to prejudge, however strong the grounds of my suspicion.

Lady Cyp. Sir Oliver, we do not think alike, and therefore with your leave we'll cut this subject short. Emily will retire—a little recollection will be useful to shew the error of some rash opinions and amend them. Go, child, remember I have now a right to look for the obedience of a daughter.

Emily. And I to expect the mildness of a mother.
                                        [*Exit.*

Lady Cyp. And now, Sir Oliver, with your permission I will dispatch a little business with my agent, and leave you to fulfil your promise to that young man, who I perceive is waiting to approach you. Follow me, Mr Earling.

            [*Exeunt Lady* CYPRESS *and* EARLING.

Sir Oliv. See here a sample of the blessings of dependance!—Poor orphan Emily, 'tis now my turn to prove that I am worthy to be call'd friend of thy gallant father.

            ALGERNON *appears.*

Oh! come in, come in, young man! I promis'd you a hearing, and I'll make good my word; but as my mind is press'd with many matters, be short and to the point.—

                                        Alg.

Alg. I will. Your nephew has had an affair with Mr. Algernon, and is wounded. You have vifited him no doubt. Has he related to you the particulars of that unpleafant bufinefs?

Sir Oliv. Before I anfwer, let me know who it is that queftions me.

Alg. My father lives upon the lands of Sir George Algernon, and I have fome acquaintance with his fon, the perfon whofe unlucky chance it was to wound your nephew.

Sir Oliv. And what's your motive for the queftion that you now put to me?

Alg. I am no ftranger to your character, and if you know the circumftances of that duel, I truft you will not fuffer Mr. Earling to mifreprefent them to the Lady Cyprefs.

Sir Oliver. Certainly I fhou'd not, if I knew the truth, fuffer it to be difguis'd; but I have no particulars from my nephew. The affair remains a myftery. Can you develope it?

Alg. If Lady Cyprefs will permit me to ftay this night, as fhe has promis'd, and you can bring me to an explanation with her in your prefence, I can fo far elucidate this myftery, that if you ftill perfift to trace it home you fhall have full poffeffion of the means.

Sir Oliv. I hardly fhould expect it at your hands; nor where my nephew's honour is concern'd fhall I be eafily induc'd to liften to other evidence than that of facts, incontrovertibly attefted, and (I am free to fay) admitted on his part.

Alg. 'Tis to fuch facts and fuch authorities I fhall appeal.

Sir Oliv. And do you mean to criminate my nephew?

Alg. Pardon me, fir, I have no other meaning but to declare the truth.

Sir Oliv. Have you the means to know it? Was you prefent at the rencontre?

Alg. If it appears that I have not the means to know the truth, or knowingly difguife it, treat me as I deferve; I'm in your hands.

Sir Oliv. Well, fir, I'll urge no further queftions on you, but ufe my intereft with the Lady Cyprefs to procure you the interview you wifh. Now fail not on your part: you know me, fir; I truft to you unknown.

Alg. Poor as I feem, I have a foul within that never yet was tainted by difhonour.

[*Exeunt feverally.*

END OF ACT III.

❀❀❀❀❀❀❀❀❀❀❀❀❀❀❀❀❀❀

ACT IV.

Lady CYPRESS, EMILY FITZALLAN, *and* EARLING.

Lady CYPRESS.

WELL, child, I have here the inftrument, that makes you rich above the dreams of avarice. I have not executed it, for that depends on you; I have not cancell'd it, becaufe this gentleman, your fteady friend, has interceded with me to recal you once more to recollection and atonement.

Emily.

Emily. For what muft I atone ?

Lady Cyp. For your intemperate defence of Algernon. Guilty or innocent, no more of him !
Where I beftow my fortune I expect to find no
oppofition to my will in the difpofal of it.

Emily. What is your will in that refpect ?

Lady Cyp. This is my will—If Lionel Montrath
furvives his wound, he is the man I deftine for my
heirefs. To this if you declare inftant affent I fhall
as inftantly confirm this paper ; if not, I cancel it,
and caft you off.

Emily. Not all the world cou'd bribe me to do
that, before I know which is the offending party.
What bafenefs, what ingratitude were mine, to give
give my hand to him that wrong'd the brave preferver of my life and honour !

Lady Cyp. Obftinate girl, you have no fuch
preferver. Have not I told you it was mere collufion ?

Emily. Madam, you have ; but I am not convinc'd, becaufe you told me fo by your attorney,
not from your own knowledge and conviction.

Lady Cyp. What will convince you ?

Emily. Proof well eftablifhed, and all parties
heard.

Lady Cyp. You to make terms that call'd yourfelf my daughter ! Where is your duty ?

Emily. Inviolate, unbroken:—I fhall ever bear
you refpect and true devotion for your goodnefs ;
but no parent, no patronefs, not even my father,
to whofe awful fpirit I now appeal, cou'd have the
power, or cou'd poffefs the right to tear away
affections from my heart, which honour, gratitude,

have

have planted there, or force me to confpire with that bad man in ftripping Algernon of fame and fortune, and fixing artifice, deceit, and murder upon a man fo near to you in blood, in nature fo abhorrent of thofe crimes:

Lady Cyp. You are mad; I have done with you; I caft you off. Now, Mr. Earling, take away your papers; they, or the thanklefs object they allude to, muft be entirely chang'd before I fign them.

[*Exit.*

Earl. Mifs Emily, it grieves me to the heart to have heard what now has pafs'd. Indeed you wrong me if you fuppofe I am the author of this fatal breach. I am no otherwife the enemy of Mr. Algernon than as I am your friend; in very truth I'm not his enemy,

Emily. Sir, for your enmity to Mr. Algernon, and fo much of your friendfhip as flows from it, I pray you let them go together; I have no ufe for either.

Earl. Do you fcorn me becaufe I pity you?

Emily. You pity me! There cannot be that ftate of human wretchednefs which cou'd reduce me to accept your pity. I wonder you can wafte your time with one, who neither courts your favour, fears your power, nor credits your profeffions.

Earl. Well, haughty madam, I have been a friend, and I can be a foe.   [*Exit.*

ALGERNON *enters.*

Alg. My Emily, my angel, what is this I've heard? Difcarded, difinherited—and for your ge-nerofity to me.

Emily. Yes, Algernon, I'm poor, but free. I was
a prifoner

a prifoner in a gaudy cage, where they wou'd fain have taught me to call names, and whiftle to a tune of Earling's making; but being a bad bird, and obftinate, my keeper let me fly; and now I've got the wide world for my portion, and nothing but my own fmall wits to truft to for picking up a living.

Alg. Fly to me, perch on my breaft, for in my heart you'll find both fhelter and affećtion.

Emily. Ah, that is generous, gallant, like your-felf; but 'tis not yet a time for me to hear you. The afylum that you offer is attack'd, the very citadel of your life and honour is befieg'd by af-failants, and you muft beat them off, my hero, or I have facrific'd myfelf to ruin without the enjoy-ment of that honeft pride which glories in the caufe for which it fuffers.

Alg. Doubt me not, Emily, the fhield of truth covers my breaft, and I'm invulnerable.

Emily. Earling accufes you of a collufion with my unknown affailant in the wood—

Alg. I'm arm'd againft that charge.

Emily. And for your wounding of Montrath, he calls it affaffination—There I fhou'd fear you are not fo well arm'd, having no feconds to appeal to, and therefore more expos'd to his attack.

Alg. Let him come on ; at all points I defy him. Now, my fweet advocate, repofe in peace, and wait the event.

Emily. Farewell ! If I am ruin'd in the caufe of truth I'll not regret the facrifice.   [*Exit.*

Alg. Heroic Emily, how I adore you—Hah! Jerry, whence come you ?

JERRY

JERRY SCUD *enters.*

Scud. From the Canaries, where the illuftrious major-domo governs, and drinking is a duty by the laws of the fage Solon of the cellars, the profound Diogenes of the tubs, of whofe academy I am a member.

Alg. You've not betray'd me in your cups, I hope.

Scud. Betray'd you! no, if you had fir'd the houfe, burnt the old lady in it, and violated the virgin purity of dame Buckram, I'd not betray you—D—n it! I fcorn a fneaker; I loath him worfe than phyfic—Go on, my boy, and fear not— I am fteady.

Alg. Pretty well for that. You've had a fip or two with honeft Simon.

Scud. Simon's a fifh; Dame Buckram is a leech; fills where fhe faftens, and delights in fuction: I honour her for her abforbent qualities, and I pronounce that they are filly apes and ignoramuffes that fay wine gets into the head—'tis falfe—I fay it gets into the heart; it drives ill humour, melancholy, treafon, and a whole gang of cowardly companions out of a man, as a carminative does crudities and indigeftion: it wou'd have fet my conftitution clear, only there's one thing fticks—

Alg. What's that, my honeft fellow? Out with it.

Scud. Why then 'tis jealoufy—and that you know is a confounded fpafm—

Alg. Away with it at once! Why, man, you don't know half your happinefs; you have the beft wife in the country—Oh! if you cou'd have heard her pine for you laft night; fhe wou'dn't hear of comfort—

E

Scud.

Scud. Indeed, indeed ! May I believe you, fquire ? May I be fure I'm not the horned beaft ?

Alg. None of my making, Jerry, on my honour.

Scud. O jubilate ! then I kick the clouds. Good bye, good bye to you. Let me embrace you. All luck attend you. I'm going to my lady; if I can throw in a provocative to ftir her in your favour I will do it ; I will upon my foul ! Good bye to you !

Alg. Stop, Jerry; hold your hand, my gallant fellow ! I am too much your friend to let you go to Lady Cyprefs in your prefent ftate. Why, man, you are tipfey.

Scud. Say drunk, and you'll not fay more than is true ; but then it is I cure my patients; when I am only fober I let them cure themfelves.   [*Exit.*

Alg. Well, get you gone ; I am not bound to find reafon for him that will not keep his own.

[*Exit* ALG.

SCENE *changes.*

Lady CYPRESS, RACHEL WILLIAMS.

Lady Cyp. Come hither, Rachel, I wou'd fpeak with you. When I promoted you to be about the perfon of Mifs Emily Fitzallan, it was becaufe I faw you was attached to her, and I was willing to do her a grace by thus preferring you. If you muft now fall back into your ftation, it is not that I have withdrawn my favour from you, but from your miftrefs.

Rachel. I know it, madam; all your people know it, for Mr. Earling has announc'd it to us; but I muft beg your ladyfhip to excufe me if I decline all fervice but Mifs Emily's.

Lady

Lady Cyp. What fhou'd enable her to keep a fervant ?

Rachel. Then fhe will ftand in the more need of me ; I'll work my fingers to the bone to ferve her. Your ladyfhip may turn me from your doors, but I will fay that Mr. Earling's a bafe cruel man, and when he has driven all your relations from you, your ladyfhip will find your houfe a defert, and nothing but a villain left within it. [*Exit.*

Lady Cyp. Out of my fight ! begone ! Such infolence is not to be endur'd—yet Earling is to blame to publifh this to all my family. So ! what comes next ?

(Mrs. BUCKRAM enters.)

Buck. Madam, I've ferv'd your ladyfhip too long to bear the arrogance of Mr. Earling. I beg to be difcharg'd ; I'll not live in the houfe with one who drives Mifs Emily out of your doors, tells fuch monftrous lies of Mr. Algernon, and fets your ladyfhip againft all your friends and relations.

Lady Cyp. Who made you a judge in matters that concern me only ? When you are cool I'll hear you. I know you have been junketing and caballing with Rachel Williams, and the reft of them—prythee retire !

Buck. That's what I mean to do, and others befide me, or I'm miftaken. We refpect your ladyfhip, but we can't put up with your attorney. [*Exit.*

(EARLING enters whilft this is faying.)

Lady Cyp. There, Mr. Earling, you hear what is faid againft you — Murmurs, complaints, invectives from all quarters—

Earl. No wonder, when that Henry Scudamore,

whom

whom I fufpect to be a fecret agent of your un-
worthy nephew's, fets them on to blacken and
arraign me.   Madam, he has had the infolence to
give me the worft of names.

Lady Cyp. Then give him his difmiffion—fend
him away at once.

Earl. It fhall be done.   [*Exit* EARLING.

Lady Cyp. Oh, that Sir Oliver had poftpon'd his
vifit to his nephew but one hour !

SCUD *appears.*

Ah, prythee, prythee, do not plague me now.
What brings you hither ?

Scud. Duty, my lady, duty—want to hear how
the draughts have agreed.

Lady Cyp. 'Tis plain how your draughts have
agreed—the operation's vifible ; no matter about
mine.

Scud. Oh pardon me, there is great matter—
fpar'd for no pains—employ'd the beft of drugs—
hope I have given content—but rumours fly—no
parrying defamation—a man may be accus'd behind
his back, and who can ftand it ?

Lady Cyp. What rumours do you allude to ?
Who has accus'd you ?

Scud. I don't know who may have accus'd me,
my lady ; I wifh to heaven I cou'd fay I have accus'd nobody.

Lady Cyp. What do you mean ?

Scud. Oh dear, madam, I am troubled with the
heart-ache ; I have a lacerated confcience.

Lady Cyp. You have a loaded head, I perceive ;
more wine in it than wit.

9

Scud.

Scud. True, my lady; it is fo full I can no longer hide the truth within it. Out it muft come, and true it is, I have flander'd Mr. Algernon. He fav'd my life, and I have ftabb'd his character.

Lady Cyp. You don't know what you fay— you're tipfey.

Scud. I wifh I had been tipfey when I fpoke of him; then I fhou'd have told the truth.

Lady Cyp. Go your ways; get you gone! a man that is in two ftories fhou'd be credited for neither. You made him out to me a compound of all vices.

Scud. That was the very vileft compound that ever came out of my hands; but lawyer Earling put a lie into my mouth, and like a gilded pill of loathfome quality I fwallow'd it, and now it makes me fick.

Lady Cyp. Begone! I will no longer be infulted with your apothecary's jargon. Never enter my doors again.

Scud. I hope your ladyfhip will give me leave to enter my own. Oh honefty, honefty! it's very pleafant to fpeak the truth, but a man is fure to lofe his cuftomers by it. [*Exit* SCUD.

(SIMON SINGLE *enters.*)

Lady Cyp. Heyday, Simon! and you too! I'll have my cellar doors wall'd up, if I am to be troubled with all the tipfey companions that refort to them.

Simon. Venerable lady, I am not inebriated. What I may be, if you wall up your cellar doors, and me within them, I can't pretend to fay. I may in that cafe drink to fupport life, as I have now been tafting a glafs, by your permiffion, to celebrate this mournful feftival.

Lady Cyp. How can it be a feftival and mournful? You know not what you fay.

Simon. Pardon me, pardon me, moft incomparable lady. A feftival it muft be, becaufe you are pleas'd to order us to be merry—Mournful it furely is, becaufe your attorney makes us fad.

Lady Cyp. You fee he is in my intereft, and you are all in league againft him.

Simon. No, no, no, my lady; 'tis not becaufe he is in your intereft we are leagued againft him—your intereft has been ever dearer to me than my own. If you turn me out of your doors this night, I can lay my hand upon my heart, and appeal to the Giver of it, that I never wrong'd you of a farthing; and, tho' a poor fervant, fcorn to cringe and lie and vilify an abfent man, as he has done. Madam, you are abus'd; the county wou'd rife up againft him, if they knew what he has faid of Mr. Algernon—fo much is your nephew belov'd.

Lady Cyp. Come, come, I know who tells you fo —'tis Henry Scudamore, and no one elfe.

Simon. Pray, madam, be no more deceiv'd, but hear and judge for yourfelf. If it was the laft word I had to utter, I wou'd fay, and fay it to his face, that lawyer Earling is a falfifier and a defamer.

Lady Cyp. Go, ftop him from difcharging Henry Scudamore; don't let him leave the houfe till I have feen him.   [*Exeunt feverally.*

SCENE *changes.*

EARLING *enters.*

Earl. Where is this Henry Scudamore ? I've hunted the whole houfe over for the fellow. If he is not driven out before this night, my poft will not be tenable to-morrow; we fhall have Algernon, brought in in triumph upon the fhoulders of his partifans, and all my labours blafted in a moment. Hah ! here's the man of all men for my purpofe ; this furly fellow has the maftiff's property; fhew him his prey, and he will faften on it—

FRANK *enters.*

Come hither, Frank ; a word with you.

Frank. What is your pleafure, mafter ?

Earl. Do you know a loofe fellow, an interloper that came to feek a place, but brought no. character; a vagabond it fhou'd feem, that calls himfelf Henry Scudamore ?

Frank. Yes, I know Henry Scudamore.

Earl. Well, honeft Frank, you fee that he came here for no good purpofe; and it is not fit he fhou'd be let to ftay and take the bread out of the mouths of better than himfelf.

Frank. There's bread enough for all of us methinks.

Earl. What then ? what then ? you're not a man, we'll hope, to be afraid of fuch a wafer cake as he is, Frank.

Frank. I'm afraid of no man.

Earl. Why then, my hearty Frank, I give you orders to turn him bodily out of this houfe, for which I have my lady's authority.

Frank.

Frank. What has he done that I fhou'd turn him out ?

Earl. He has infulted me, traduç'd my character, and fet me at defiance.

Frank. Has he done this ?

Earl. He has.

Frank. Then let him ftay for me—I will not touch him ; I honour him for his fpirit. They call me furly Frank, and fo. I am if any man affronts me ;' but I'll be no attorney's catch-pole, lookye ! And as for turning out, if that's your game, there's but one man I'll do that office for, and that's yourfelf, my mafter—There you have it.　[*Exit.*

Earl. Impudent varlet ! the contagion's general if he has caught it. The whole fwarm 's upon me, and I muft ftand their buzzing ; as for their ftings I'm not in fear of them fo long as I can keep the queen of the hive in my poffeffion.

(ALGERNON *enters.*)

Oho ! I have lit upon you at laft. Harkye, fir, you Henry Scudamore, whom nobody knows, decamp, pack up your wallet, and betake yourfelf nobody cares whither. Off ! the Lady Cyprefs warns you off—begone !

Alg. Go back and fay to Lady Cyprefs, when fhe fends her warning by a proper meffenger, I will obey her.

Earl. Why, who am I ? What do you take me for ?

Alg. A wretch beneath my notice—a defamer.

(SIMON *enters.*)

Simon. Well met, friend Henry, 'tis my lady's orders

orders that you don't leave the houfe 'till fhe has feen you.

Earl. Sot, you are drunk. You never had fuch orders.

Simon. I had no orders—very well! And I'm a fot, I'm drunk—why, very well!—So much for me, now for yourfelf—you are no fot; you're fober Mr. Earling the attorney; you're never drunk, for no man will drink with you; you never make miftakes about your orders, for you are under orders from the old one never to fpeak the truth, and faithfully adhere to your inftructions.

Earl. This to my face?

Simon. Oh yes, I never faw a face better intitled to the compliment. I only wifh to fee it face to face with Harry Algernon, and then perhaps your face may be promoted, where I may treat it with an egg or two.

Alg. Go, go, unhappy man; it can't be pleafant to hear yourfelf defcrib'd fo faithfully.

Earl. I'll not go—I fummon you before the Lady Cyprefs—fhe'll do me juftice—fhe'll avenge my wrongs. Here comes Sir Oliver—I appeal to him.

(Sir OLIVER *enters.)*

Sir Oliv. What is the matter?

Earl. Thefe fellows have infulted me moft grofsly.

Sir Oliv. You are a lawyer. You have your redrefs.

Earl. Sir, 'tis above redrefs by any law.

Sir Oliv. Then put it up and feek redrefs from patience. That is a remedy for all complaints.

Earl. I hope I've better remedies than patience —I warrant I'll exterminate thefe infolents. I'll
pluck

pluck 'em root and branch out of this houfe, and hurl 'em to the dunghill that they fprung from.

Sir Oliv. Go then and fet about it. Leave me, fir, I've bufinefs with this gentleman.

Earl. This gentleman, forfooth! this gentle-man—   [*Exit.*

Simon. Well, he may be a gentleman for me, only he lets the bottle ftand too long, and takes no pity on his company, that wifh to give it motion— that's not quite like a gentleman methinks—elfe he may be a fober fort of a gentleman—but not a lord—no, no, at leaft he'll never be as drunk as a lord.   [*Exit.*

Sir Oliv. Now, fir, I've feen my nephew fince we laft convers'd. You afk'd me then if I had been inform'd of the particulars of that rencontre, and by the motives you affign'd for the enquiry, I fhou'd fuppofe you know fome circumftances of that dark affair.

Alg. The whole correctly.

Sir Oliv. Indeed! I hardly fhou'd have thought that Mr. Algernon wou'd have reveal'd the whole to any but his neareft and moft confidential friend.

Alg. Nor has he; it remains ftill in his bofom an inviolable fecret, though known to me.

Sir Oliv. You mean to fay that fecrets in your keeping are fecure. I have my nephew's ftory as you have Algernon's, and fhou'd be glad, with your confent, to compare them with each other.

Alg. They cannot differ, for my account is drawn up by your nephew, and being fign'd by him, he neither can, nor will depart from it.

                                                      Sir

Sir Oliv. You much amaze me, fir, that Mr. Algernon fhou'd give a paper of fuch confequence out of his hand. I greatly wifh to fee it.

Alg. Wou'd it relieve your mind at the fame time to fee and talk with Algernon himfelf?

Sir Oliv. Oh infinitely, if I cou'd obtain it.

Alg. Then with a man of honour 'twou'd be mean to trifle any longer—I am Algernon.

Sir Oliv. How!—Algernon!—may I believe you?—

Alg. You fhall not doubt me—There's your nephew's paper—No eye but your's has feen it from my hand.

Sir Oliv. Sir!—Mr. Algernon—I afk your pardon—I am fatisfied—but can you be unknown, and in this houfe?

Alg. I never enter'd it before this day, nor to my knowledge ever faw my aunt 'till I appear'd before her in this habit, which I fhall now put off—but hark! we fhall be interrupted here—Can't we retire to a more private place?

Sir Oliv. To my apartment—if you'll be pleas'd to follow me.—Ah! fir, ah! Mr. Algernon, how hard to find, now at the clofe of a long life of fervices, all it's enjoyments, all it's labours loft.

END OF ACT IV.

✕✕✕✕✕✕✕✕✕✕✕✕✕✕✕✕✕✕✕✕✕✕

A C T V.

SCENE, *the Caſtle Hall.*

JERRY SCUD *and* JENNY.

SCUD.

WELL, well, well! jewel Jenny, here we are
for the laſt time: farewell viſits, to be ſure,
are melancholy matters; but we have many good
friends in the caſtle ſtill, and tho' I am thrown out
of the cabinet, I have kept up my intereſt in the
kitchen.

Jenny. Aye, and in the county too, when it
ſhall be known that you have forfeited my lady's
favour by ſpeaking up for Mr. Algernon; he is ſo
much pitied and belov'd by all men, that your
neighbours will ſham ſick on purpoſe to employ
you.

Scud. To ſay the truth, I have ſometimes thought
that was my lady's only complaint; but I took care
my phyſic ſhould not cure her of it; and my comfort is that nobody of the faculty will profit by my
loſs; for when ſhe leaves off my medicines ſhe'll find
herſelf too well to employ a doctor.

Jenny. Come, come, Jerry, ſhe'll not leave off
you nor your medicines. If you can get to the
ſpeech of her, a little coaxing, and a ſubmiſſive
apology, will ſet all things right.

Scud. No, no, jewel Jenny, ſhe'll hear no apology,
and therefore I have expreſs'd myſelf more at large

in

in my bill—Here it is, here it is—It's a bouncer;
isn't it?

Jenny. Yes, marry, if fhe has patience to go
through this fhe'll find you have enough to fay
for yourfelf; but I fufpect, Jerry, this argument is
a little too much on one fide.

Scud. Turn over the leaf, and you'll find a great
deal more on the other fide.

SIMON SINGLE *and Mrs.* DOROTHY BUCKRAM.
Ah my good friends, my good friends! this is
the moft doleful vifit I ever made to the caftle.
Jenny can witnefs I have pafs'd a fleeplefs night:
that incubus of an attorney rode upon me like the
night-mare.

Buck. Rode indeed! Set a beggar on horfeback,
and where will he not ride?

Scud. I attempted to put a cracker under his
tail, but it burft in my hand, and I only burnt my
own fingers without finging him.

Simon. Let him go; the road he travels is all
down-hill, and when he comes to his journey's end,
he'll find thofe that will put crackers enough under
his tail, I warrant me.

Dor. As for me, a jackdaw in a cage has a better
life of it than I have, for he may cry rogue, and not
be chidden for it—We fhall all be turn'd away:
I lay my account to be fent going for one.

Simon. Thirty years I have pafs'd within thefe
walls, and I would fooner pafs the reft of my days
within the walls of a prifon than live in a houfe
where fcurrility is carefs'd and plain fpeaking
turn'd out of doors—Hah! who comes here?

ALGERNON

ALGERNON *enters in his own Dreſs.*

Buck. Bleſs the good mark! our Henry—No—Yes, ſure 'tis Henry; how comes this to paſs?

Alg. I'm order'd to attend upon my lady, ſo I put on my beſt.

Simon. Hark ye, my friend, if it is not your own, bad is your beſt. Let us have no falſe feathers. Where did you get this ſuit?

Alg. 'Tis Harry Algernon's. He and I wear the ſame cloaths: one tailor ſerves us both—Isn't it true, Jerry?

Scud. It is, it is, and the ſame meaſure fits you.

Simon. I don't know what you mean.

Alg. Then I'll inform you. Here are but two of you in company that do not know me; you are both my friends, my generous, zealous friends, for which I thank you, and come in perſon hither to convince you that Algernon is not that worthleſs man, which calumny has painted him to be.

Buck. Heaven's grace light on you, if indeed you are that injur'd gentleman.

Scud. Oh by my ſoul, he is the very man: you may take that upon my word for truth.

Simon. I ſaw it; I ſaid it; I knew he was a gentleman. Now we have got that attorney in a trap.

Jenny. Yes, yes, he'll make that Earling ſhrink into his hole.

Simon. Hang him, polecat, I'll ſmoke him out of it. Oh! the inconceivable lies that miſcreant has told of a gentleman he does not know even by ſight. I pray you, ſir, don't diſcover yourſelf to him, till we have had him up before my lady—

Methinks

Methinks I hear her fay, Simon, I am convinc'd that lawyer is a rafcal—Turn him out!

Buck. Aye, we'll all lend a helping hand to that.

Scud. Yes, or a helping foot, if that is wanted. I have one at his fervice.

Simon. Blefs you, my worthy mafter, blefs you heartily! I hope I have faid nothing to affront you; I was a little by the head juft now, but that's over.

Alg. So is not my remembrance. I fhall ever prize you as my beft of friends.

Simon. Lord love you, we are all your friends; we are all Algernons and Anti Earlings.

Buck. And when the election comes, we'll wear your colours.

Scud. Only put me in office on that day: let me be furgeon-general to the enemy, and I'll engage they fhall have more freeholders in the hofpital than at the huftings. I'll fcour their confciences, I warrant me.

Alg. Now, my good friends, keep fecret what has pafs'd, and wait the event in filence—Here comes one, a gentle advocate, whom I would fain fpeak to apart.

Simon. We are gone; we are gone! All happinefs befal you! 			[*Exeunt all but* ALGERNON.

EMILY FITZALLAN *enters.*

Emily. Blefs me! you've chang'd your habit.

Alg. Yes, my charmer—In chace 'tis lawful to hang out falfe colours, but when we are clear'd and going into action we muft fhew what we are.

Emily.

Emily. Right, and where truth unfolds her ftand-ard, victory muft follow.

Alg. And what fhould follow victory? What but the glorious prize for which I ftruggle? that prize which fortune, aiming to impoverifh, has only made more rich in my efteem—that generous heart, that facrific'd for me intereft, for which fo many facrifice themfelves.   Now call to mind thofe words fo hea-venly fweet, which you left with me, whilft the in-genuous blufh glow'd on your cheek—" Henry, I " live for you !"

Emily. Ah! that was then the only way I had to reinftate you in your property; and, tho' it coft a blufh to fay thofe words, ftill I could fay them, for I fcorn'd to rob you—but to repeat them now wou'd be—Oh heaven!—it would be every thing but falfe, my Henry.

Alg. Then let me take that truth into a heart, of which no human power can difpoffefs you.

Emily. I hope not, Henry, for take that away and I am poor indeed.

Alg. 'Tis your's for ever—and believe me, dear one, if my too credulous aunt has not outliv'd her reafon, fhe will fee the injuftice of her own decifions and revoke them.   For my exclufion fhe may have fome plea; our families have been at fuit for years, and law will cut afunder clofer ties than thofe exift-ing between her and me; but of her motives for difcarding you, take my word, Emily, fhe'll foon repent.

Emily. It is not that I fear her worthlefs favour-ite; the wretch has brought a ftorm upon his head, and has already had fome heavy fhocks—but my worft fears point to another quarter.   *Alg*.

Alg. I underſtand you. 'Tis Montrath you dread.

Emily. I could not temporize; I ſpoke too plainly. Indignant of the claim ſhe made upon me, I ſet her power too boldly at defiance, and challeng'd her to cancel her bequeſt.

Alg. You muſt conſult Sir Oliver upon this: I cannot ſpeak upon Montrath's affair even to you.

Emily. I ſee you either cannot or you will not, therefore I aſk no queſtions, well perſuaded you never would take arms againſt the life of any man and know yourſelf in fault.

Alg. I hope I ſhan't be found to have ſo done—but look! here comes Sir Oliver.—I'll leave you; he may perhaps be leſs reſerv'd than I am.

[*Exit* ALGERNON.

Sir OLIVER MONTRATH *enters.*

Sir Oliv. Was not that Algernon?

Emily. You know him, ſir, it ſeems—

Sir Oliv. I think I do; I have cauſe to know him.

Emily. Ah, ſir, you ſpeak ſo mournfully, I fear you have found no comfort in your viſit to your nephew.

Sir Oliv. Small comfort—Yet the danger of his wound is much abated.

Emily. Then I'm afraid you have, or think you have, ſome cauſe of anger againſt Algernon.

Sir Oliv. No, Emily, no anger againſt him. You cannot think too well of Algernon, tho' I could wiſh you had not put your thoughts in language quite ſo warm.

Emily. 'Twas indiſcreet, but that defamer urg'd me, and put me off my guard.

F

Sir Oliv. Cou'dn't you find another and a ftronger caufe that put you off your guard ? Is there not a certain paffion, which our hearts are fubject to, that neither keeps a guard upon itfelf, nor fuffers any to be kept againft it ?

Emily. If I fhould anfwer that as truth would prompt me, fhou'dn't I expofe myfelf to another reproof for want of caution ?

Sir Oliv. No ; for fo far from thinking with my lady, that you have chofen ill, I think with you that you could no where make a better choice—And more than this—was your brave father living, and knew what I know of your Algernon, he would approve your judgment.

Emily. As I am fure you would not give that name but to a facred truth, what you have faid fanctions the character of Algernon—but does it warrant me in fuffering him to make a facrifice of intereft by marrying a beggar ?

Sir Oliv. You point the queftion wrong, and fhould have afk'd if it exculpates me, your father's friend, for fuffering you to call yourfelf a beggar.— No, my dear child, it does not, nor will I permit it to be faid, the daughter of the generous Fitzallan, who in the battle found me faint with wounds, and whilft he cover'd me receiv'd his death, wanted that drofs which I abounded in.—This, Emily, this never fhould be faid ; fo come with me, and don't oppofe one word to my refolves ; for in an act of honour I will paufe at no man's bidding, no, my pretty one, nor yet at any woman's, tho' grac'd with all the charms that heaven can give her. [*Exeunt.*

6

SCENE

SCENE *changes.*

EARLING *alone.*

Now, fortune, one kind lift, and I am landed. So far fuccefs goes with me: I have nothing more to fear from Emily; that pert proud mifs is filenc'd and thrown by. It now remains to fweep thofe menial vermin out my way, thofe infects that annoy me: old Sir Oliver, that blufters about juftice, is a hypocrite; he cannot be a friend to Algernon; and yet he troubles me, takes up my feat at table, occupies the ear of the old lady, and obftructs my fuit, which ftood fo fair, that if I could but feize one lucky moment, one fair opportunity. —Hah! I have found it.—Here fhe comes alone —Now, impudence befriend me!

Lady CYPRESS *enters.*

Lady Cyp. So, Mr. Earling! much as I love peace, I will not purchafe it by mean conceffions; I will not fuffer the gentleman I efteem and truft to be affronted by my fawcy fervants; they fhall atone, or troop.

Earl. Moft amiable, moft excellent of ladies, whom with my heart I ferve, honour, obey and worfhip; I want words to fpeak my gratitude.—Thus at your feet in humble adoration let me feal on this dear hand the pledge, the facred pledge, of my unutterable, my unbounded love.

SIMON *and* DOROTHY *enter.*

Simon. Look, Dorothy, the devil's at his prayers.

Dor. I hope they're his laft prayers.

Earl. Curfe on their coming! what a moment loft! Madam, do you permit your menial fervants thus to break in upon your private moments?

Lady

Lady Cyp. Why not? If you have any thing to add to your laſt ſpeech I ſhall not interrupt it. You may reſume your poſture, and go on.

Earl. Madam, I cannot.

Lady Cyp. I can help your memory if you have loſt the word. 'Twas *love, unbounded love.* When you had gone ſo far out of all bounds, all meaſure of reſpect, can the appearance of theſe ſilly people deter you from proceeding?

Earl. Madam, if you're offended, I have done. I'll humbly take my leave.

Lady Cyp. No, ſir, I muſt inſiſt upon your ſtaying. Tho' you are foil'd to add a ſingle word to inſolence ſo perfect and complete, yet you ſhall not be robb'd of your juſt right, that nature gives you, to be heard in vindication of your own aſſertions. If you have ſpoke the truth, and nothing but the truth, of Algernon, his character cannot be reſcued, let the fate of your's be what it may.

Simon. Any thing the matter, Mr. Attorney? Afraid you are not quite well juſt now. You look a little pale.

Lady Cyp. Hold your tongue, fooliſh fellow! you, Simon, in the firſt place, and you next, miſtreſs, who dare to tell me I am made the dupe of falſe impreſſions, are you not both aſham'd to look this injur'd gentleman in the face?

Simon. It is a face to make a man aſham'd, and we did bluſh to ſee him on his knees before your ladyſhip.

Lady Cyp. That's my affair, fall down on your's and aſk forgiveneſs of him.

Simon. Pray, madam, don't command me to do that,

that, for fear I never fhould forgive myfelf.—I afk your pardon for approaching you when I was tipfey, but you bade me drink, and I was over eager to obey you.

Lady Cyp. That's eafily forgiven; but your abufe of this gentleman, whom I muft ftill call the friend of truth, is monftrous.

Simon. Madam, if that gentleman is the friend of truth, he makes very free with his friend truly. I only faid he told lies to your ladyfhip, that's no abufe, for here come thofe can prove it.

Sir OLIVER MONTRATH *and* EMILY.

Earl. My evil genius! what does he do here?

Sir Oliv. Forgive me, my good lady, if I come to atone to you and this fair advocate for my unjuft fufpicions of your nephew. I have one here waiting, who'll confront that gentleman, his accufer, and, I truft, remove fome falfe impreffions that your ladyfhip may have imbibed from his unfounded charges. Come in, fir, if you pleafe.

ALGERNON *enters.*

Lady Cyp. How now! who's this? Henry!

Sir Oliv. I claim your promife to give him hearing.

Earl. I proteft againft him; that fellow's an impoftor: we fhall not liften to his evidence.

Lady Cyp. He firft came here humbly to afk for fervice, pleaded decay, and faid he was a gentleman by birth; I pitied him, and offer'd him relief. He now has chang'd his drefs, fhifted his character, and claims to be an advocate for Algernon. Thefe are fufpicious circumftances, and I fhou'd have fome better reafons for believing him than I am yet poffefs'd of. Do you know any fuch, Sir Oliver?

Earl.

Earl. Aye, fir, do you know who this champion is ?

Sir Oliv. Sir, give me leave to afk—Do you ?

Earl. Not I; I know him not.

Sir Oliv. Yet you know Algernon, are intimate
with all his habits, frailties, faults, offences—have
look'd into his heart, and kindly told the fecrets
you difcover'd.—Oh thou flanderer ! Now look him
in the face, and prove your charge.—Well may
you ftart—Mark his confufion, madam !—This is
your nephew, this is Algernon.

Emily. Yes, on my honour, and my brave preferver.

Lady Cyp. I am confounded.—Where is that defamer ?

Simon. Madam, he has ftept afide to mend a
flaw in his indictment.—How do you do, Mr. Attorney ? Come forward, if you pleafe, and get ac-
quainted with this gentleman's face. You knew
him well enough behind his back.

Lady Cyp. Peace ! let me hear what Algernon
will fay in his own caufe.

Sir Oliv. Speak for yourfelf, brave Algernon.

Alg. I am that exil'd man, whom, on the word
of this defamer, tho' unknown to him even by fight,
it feems, you have profcrib'd. Defpairing of admiffion to your prefence, and driven in felf-defence
on this refource, I took a counterfeited character,
and faw what I had never been allow'd to approach—
your perfon. Much I wifh'd to fpeak in mitiga-
tion of your prejudice, and give a plain recital of
my wrongs; but you had then no ear for fuch dif-
courfe, and I was told to wait your better leifure.

Lady.

Lady Cyp. All this is true—proceed.

Alg. A friend here prefent told me I was accus'd to you of various crimes and grofs enormities. I plead to failings, to the common errors and indifcretions youth is fubject to, but, I truft, I have never degraded my character or debas'd my principle ; I am no gamefter, as he makes me to be; no diffipater of my paternal fortune, as he infinuates ; no libertine, as he afferts; and, let me add, in the hearing of Sir Oliver Montrath, I am no affaffin.

Sir Oliv. It is now my duty, and a painful one I feel it, to bring to light, in vindication of an injur'd character, the guilty perfon, for whofe fhameful act no better palliation can be found than temporary madnefs and intoxication. The monfter, from whofe brutal violence the pureft of heaven's creatures was preferv'd by Algernon, how fhall I fpeak it without fhame and horror ! was Lionel Montrath.

Lady Cyp. I am confounded and amaz'd! Montrath !—This, if not told by you, Sir Oliver, wou'd mock belief.

Sir Oliv. Your nephew was too noble to difclofe it, tho' he has in his hands a written paper fign'd by the offender for his vindication. This, I believe, he never has difcover'd, even to that lady, tho' a party in it.

Emily. Never, but conftantly evaded my enquiries.

Sir Oliv. To this when I fhall add, that my rafh nephew forc'd the duel on him in confequence of blows exchang'd between them, I truft I may with
safety

safely reft his caufe upon the facts adduc'd—unlefs indeed this gentleman has any other charge, which in his modefty he will prefer.

Earl. You'll not draw any thing from me, Sir Oliver; you may talk on; I prefer filence.

Sir Oliv. You are right; 'tis time your tongue had fome repofe.

Lady Cyp. Pray do not keep him longer in my fight. My nephew does not feem to hold him worthy of a retort.

Alg. No, madam, I have nothing to return him for his malicious flander, but my contempt.

Lady Cyp. If he can feel, 'tis punifhment enough.

Sir Oliv. Be gone! your infamy go with you; and may no part of it adhere to your profeffion.

Earl. Let my profeffion look to itfelf—There are fome underftandings in this world made, it fhould feem, by nature to be duped. Had you not been fo eafy of belief, I had not been fo forward to deceive you. Now put what name you will upon my conduct, there are fuch glaring inftances in point, of dealers in feduction, infamy, and falfe impreffions on credulity, as make my fhame no wonder.

[*Exit.*

Lady Cyp. Now, Henry, you've appeal'd to me for juftice—hear my decree. There is your deftiny; that is the prize which you have nobly earn'd, My heart, fo long eftrang'd, is now your own. You are my fon, and Emily my daughter; all I poffefs is your's—Have I aton'd?

Alg. Oh! you have given me that, which might atone for all the pains mortality cou'd feel—beauty to charm me, talents to enchant, and truth to fix my happinefs fecure.

Emily.

Emily. Oh! Henry, bear me to my benefactrefs, and let me kneel———

Lady Cyp. Yes, I will let you kneel, my child, for now thou haft a treafure worth thy thanks— Be virtuous, loving, faithful to each other; ape not the fafhions of this guilty world; feek pleafures where alone they can be found, in nuptial harmony, domeftic duties, and that fweet reflection, which fortune well employ'd is fure to give.—Rife, my adopted, rife!

Sir Oliv. Oh, let me add a bleffing—May you be—Well, well, it will not forth; my heart's too full; but I will fend it up in thought towards heaven— Here, Emily, my love, I'll put the firft chain on your bridal arm; they are pure pearls, my child; not fpoils of war, but gifts of gratitude for life preferv'd —wear them for my fake, and when I am dead caft a kind look upon them, and drop one pearly tear, richer than them all, to the memory of old Oliver.

Emily. Oh fir, fir, fir — my father and my friend— !

Sir Oliv. So, fo ! no more. Henry, my gallant boy, give me your hand—a foldier's greeting after victory—time was I could have grafp'd it harder.

Alg. I accept it, and prefs it to my heart.

Lady Cyp. Where are you all? This is a day of joy. Simon, I look to you to oil the hinges of my caftle gates, that they may open freely to the neighbours, the tenants, and the poor.

Simon. I'll make 'em fwing, fo pleafe you, and for one bad man now gone out of them, a hundred good ones fhall come in, I warrant me.

8

Lady

Lady Cyp. You, Dorothy, muſt ſet the girls à dancing; and you, Rachel, muſt lead the ball in honour of your miſtreſs.

(SCUD *and* JENNY, *who had crept in behind the ſervants, now ſtep forward.)*

Scud. And when the bumpkins caper and kick ſhins, may they not want a plaiſter, good my Lady? I'll cure them gratis on this happy night. I have brought a bill, ſo pleaſe you, that will bear ſome riders on it, and not break it's back.

Lady Cyp. We'll have no bills nor bickerings any more; and to cut ſhort all reckonings, I'll eſtabliſh you apothecary general to the caſtle upon a ſalary fixt.

Simon. Then, Jerry, the leſs phyſic you ſend in the better for yourſelf.

Scud. And for all parties, my moſt honoured lady. I hope moſt heartily for all your ſakes my place will be as near a ſinecure as poſſible.

Lady Cyp. I hope ſo too. You and your fair wife are welcome. She is a child of the caſtle, and will grace our dance.

Scud. Yes, under favour, Jenny, tho' I ſay it, has all the ſteps that now are thought ſo graceful! ſhe'll balance on one leg and ſend the other upon a cruize into her neighbour's pocket; no magnetizing doctor or dotterell-monger can ſurpaſs my Jenny for the fine attitudes.

Lady Cyp. You're a ſtrange mortal; but let mirth go round, and if the humble annals of our caſtle can cheer one honeſt, eaſe one heavy heart, our harmleſs efforts have not been in vain.

END OF THE COMEDY.

EPILOGUE.

Spoken by Miss BETTERTON.

NOW *False Impressions* are no more in view,
  Allow me to present you with the true—
A bond it is, imprefs'd by honor's seal,
With Truth's fair form, grav'd in perennial steel;
A bond of gratitude, to which I set
Both hand and heart to verify my debt;
And tho' in law an infant, and in merit
Poor, as heav'n knows, I am not poor in spirit;
I'll pay you when I'm able from my gains;
If you'll have patience, I'll not spare for pains.

  In truth I did not seek this awful post;
No champion I to face so brave a host.
There are, who when five yawning acts are o'er,
Can tickle those same yawners till they roar;
These are the friends our profing bard should court;
He gives soft slumbers, but they make the sport;
They have the spell to puff the stage balloon
Brim full of gas, and blow it to the moon:
Not so our poet—He accounts it right
To keep his critics ever in his sight;
Such jaunts might turn their brains, disturb their thinking,
And send them where they'd lose the art of finking.

  Rigour, when just, he can, he will endure,
The stream is bitter, but the spring is pure;
Candor, when candor haply he can meet,
Like Moses' rod, can turn the bitter sweet;
But the foul puddle, in which malice dips,
Is a dire dose—He spurns it from his lips.

  He writes, because, tho' writing is abus'd,
The world is not too grave to be amus'd;
He writes, and ever to some moral end,
Because the world is not too good to mend.
Soft female hearts are prone as wax to melt,
And, true or false, impreffions will be felt;
Youth's yielding clay too easily receives
The featur'd stamp that cross-ey'd cunning gives:
Therefore let her, whose dang'rous lot in life
Hangs on the balance betwixt maid and wife,
Lay those few short prescriptions to her heart,
With which the Lady Cyprefs clos'd her part;
For base seduction spreads on every side
His treach'rous snares to mesh th' unwary bride.
She, in whose eyes enticing Cupids play,
Gives impudence the clue, and leads the way.
What tho' the faithlefs husband quits her hand,
Truth, like a column, of itself can stand:
To reas'ning minds sufficient strength is giv'n,
And none but fools can charge their faults on heav'n.

———————

In the Press, and speedily will be Published,

A NEW AND COMPLETE EDITION

OF THE

O B S E R V E R,

In Six Volumes, Duodecimo,

NEWLY CLASSED AND ARRANGED;

And containing, in Addition to the Original Matter,

AN ENTIRE TRANSLATION

O F

THE CLOUDS OF ARISTOPHANES,

WITH NOTES CRITICAL AND EXPLANATORY.

Also,

A separate Edition of the said Translated COMEDY, printed on such Paper, and in such Type, as to accommodate such Purchasers or Possessors of the former Editions, as may chuse to attach it thereunto.

www.ingramcontent.com/pod-product-compliance
Lightning Source LLC
Chambersburg PA
CBHW030001030726
47499CB00008B/2844